DROW REQUIEM

DROW REQUIEM
CHRONICLES OF SHADOW BOURNE™
BOOK EIGHT

MARTHA CARR
MICHAEL ANDERLE

DISRUPTIVE IMAGINATION

This book is a work of fiction. All of the characters, organizations, and events portrayed in this novel are either products of the author's imagination or are used fictitiously. Sometimes both.

Copyright © 2024 LMBPN Publishing
Cover by Fantasy Book Design
Cover copyright © LMBPN Publishing
A Michael Anderle Production

LMBPN Publishing supports the right to free expression and the value of copyright. The purpose of copyright is to encourage writers and artists to produce the creative works that enrich our culture.

The distribution of this book without permission is a theft of the author's intellectual property. If you would like permission to use material from the book (other than for review purposes), please contact support@lmbpn.com. Thank you for your support of the author's rights.

LMBPN Publishing
2375 E. Tropicana Avenue, Suite 8-305
Las Vegas, Nevada 89119 USA

Version 1.00, September 2024
ebook ISBN: 979-8-88878-259-0
Print ISBN: 979-8-89354-269-1

The Oriceran Universe (and what happens within / characters / situations / worlds) are Copyright © 2017-2024 by Martha Carr and LMBPN Publishing.

THE DROW REQUIEM TEAM

Thanks to our JIT Readers

Diane L. Smith
Dorothy Lloyd
Jeff Goode
Sean Kesterson
Christopher Gilliard
Jan Hunnicutt

Editor

SkyFyre Editing Team

CHAPTER ONE

The ring was gone. Ellis pawed through her drawers in a panic. If she couldn't find the ring, Ilva would find some unpleasant way to kill her. She pulled out every drawer in the cabin for the third time.

"Is this a ruse to stop them from getting married?" Landon asked. He was not displaying the appropriate urgency. "Because they could probably do it without rings. It's not a legal requirement."

"I'm not trying to stop them. Will you get off your butt and help me? I had it when I woke up."

She excavated her pockets for the umpteenth time, fingers flying.

Ilva had asked Ellis to be her second at the wedding, which had taken her by surprise. Ilva had never been her biggest fan, and she had suspected her father's meddling. Connor had sworn innocence, so Ellis had agreed.

They would use a truncated version of the drow ceremony. Some customs, like the couple dissolving two ends of a tunnel until they reached each other Lady-and-the-

Tramp-style, didn't translate well to human environments, and Sebastian had promised to keel-haul them if they put a hole in his boat.

They would put on a good show, though. Rami, the head chef, was still in the medical bay after losing his hand, but he was well enough for visitors, and Emily, the acting chef, had peppered him with questions about drow weddings. She had drummed up a few bottles of mushroom wine and a traditional savory cake so the old ways would be honored, which was good. Connor and Ilva each had one foot firmly planted in tradition.

Ellis grudgingly admitted that they were good together.

When Ellis told her mother about the wedding, Claire requested shore leave. Sebastian had refused to grant it until Ellis intervened. She didn't think Claire would do anything to stop them, but she feared there might be a scene. It had been a relief when Claire's stiff figure disappeared over the horizon in the Zodiac.

The night before, the couple had slept in hammocks on the deck on opposite sides of the ship, honoring the drow tradition of a couple spending time on the surface in the wilderness before the wedding. They had emerged from their hammocks damp and salty but otherwise unharmed.

Even Val had agreed to take part in the wedding. Since they'd gotten back to the *Eel*, Val had spent a great deal of time in "conferences" with the captain. Inside the hush puppies, there was a lot of wide-mouthed shouting.

Ellis kept the void sword with her. She had tried to leave it in her cabin once while she ran a quick errand, but she had gotten feverish and disoriented before she reached the stairs. Her vision had twisted and her feet had taken her back to the cabin of their own accord. When she thought about what that meant, her mind got jumbled, and she gave up. There was a thin layer of unease beneath everything she did now, and with the dark metal scabbard against her back, she was always cold.

Ellis rubbed her hands together and went back to searching for Ilva's wedding ring.

"You should retrace your steps," Landon suggested.

"You're enjoying this," Ellis growled.

Landon shrugged, but his eyes sparkled as he helped her search the passage between her rack and the mess. The journey was fruitless, but she was glad to have his company. In the mess, she had a stroke of inspiration. "Emily, have you got shadow magic goggles back there?"

Emily, who was chopping a stack of oyster mushrooms, paused and pointed at the bulkhead. A pair of purple goggles dangled from a hook next to a row of hanging pots. "If that's all you need, take them and get out of my galley," she cheerfully requested.

Percy, who was at an island in the back of the galley peeling sweet potatoes, shot Ellis a help-me look. Rami would not be well enough to return to work for some time, and when he did come back, he would need a long period of readjustment. There was still an entire crew to feed, however, so when Percy had unwisely volunteered that he was handy with a paring knife, he had been assigned KP duty.

Ellis chucked him on the shoulder as she retrieved the goggles from their hook. "Hang in there, chef." The goggles allowed Ellis to see objects enchanted with shadow magic, which made searching the mess and passage easy.

The ring *still* wasn't there. Sighing, she returned to her cabin, where the goggles were less useful. The four crewmembers' cloakers, hush puppies, potions, and shadow-magic-infused body armor made the room light up like Las Vegas. Every time she turned her head, Ellis caught sight of the void sword in her peripheral vision, the black metal shining like a lighthouse's beacon.

Then she saw a faint purple glow under the edge of her bed. Fishing between the mattress and the bedframe, she dug out a thin stone band that gleamed with shadow magic. It was a relief to push the goggles onto her forehead. Even without them, the ring was pretty, a smooth band carved from a solid chunk of amethyst.

She triumphantly held it up to show her brother, who grinned. "That was the easy part," Landon said. "Now you've got to go attend *her*."

Ilva had wanted to hold the wedding in the engine room, which was the closest thing to a cavern on the ship. Sebastian had nixed this idea for safety reasons but had allowed Ilva and Connor to take over the cargo hold. Ellis idled in the passage but finally ran out of excuses and pushed through the doors.

Ilva, who Ellis had expected to be cross, was in good spirits. She was also resplendent in a figure-skimming crystal silk gown and wore a net veil.

"It's a proud moment in a boy's life when his parents get married. You look nice, Mom," Landon remarked.

"Oh, my gods, Ilva! Where did you get that dress?" Ellis asked.

Ilva smiled smugly. "The bosun made it for me out of discarded crystal silk armor scraps."

"You look incredible. And bulletproof."

"I am. And the veil is a fishing net that Trissa helped me gussy up with mushroom dye."

Ilva's smile was so genuine that Ellis wrapped her arms around her.

"Where is Charlie?" Ilva asked. Ellis, who hadn't seen him all morning, said she didn't know. Ilva raised an eyebrow. "Is he afraid the wedding will prove contagious?"

"What do you... Do you mean *us?*"

Ellis had no idea what Charlie thought about marriage, and there was no time to find out now. There was too much to do.

"I'm going to go check on Dad," Landon stated.

He left, and Ilva called Ellis over to where a few of the *Violet Eel* crewmembers were standing with a large tarp. Six others hung from the overhead, and Ellis helped the crew maneuver this one up and affix it to the rigging bolts.

When it was up, she stood back and admired their work. It looked like a pop art installation at a museum of contemporary art. That was the last big task; everything else was fussing. The piles of cardboard boxes along the bulkheads were bedecked with fairy lights, and Ellis went around them, replacing bulbs. There were also clear glass beakers stuffed with bioluminescent lichen that they'd begged from the science department.

Ellis wasn't good with hair, but she helped Ilva weave glowing purple trumpet mushrooms into her long braid. When she was done, Ilva grabbed her hands. "I have enjoyed becoming family," she said formally. "I look forward to making it official."

"Me too." Tears rose in Ellis' eyes. "I'm happy for you two."

Ilva sniffed. "Please do not make me cry. I am wearing Emily's eye makeup, and we have limited time."

An hour later, everyone except the skeleton crew keeping the *Violet Eel* afloat filtered into the cargo hold. Ellis nervously got Ilva settled behind the final tarp, reviewing the script for the ceremony on a sweaty piece of notebook paper.

"Ready?" Ellis asked Ilva, who nodded enthusiastically.

Ellis touched her earpiece. "Curtains up, folks."

With an embarrassed cough, Sebastian stepped onto a makeshift platform next to the tarps.

Ellis gaped, and a low chuckle rose from the crowd.

"Oh, my gods, he wore it," someone muttered.

"Is that a garment humans often wear?" Ilva whispered to Ellis.

Ellis blinked. "That's not a garment that *anyone wears.*"

Sebastian Altamont was resplendent in a seventeenth-century British naval uniform, complete with lace ruff and tricorn hat. Instead of being blue, the uniform had been dyed a garish purple. An embroidered pale lilac eel adorned the front of the hat.

"What the hell is that?" Ellis asked Emily, who was standing close enough to whisper to.

"About four years ago, Val and the skipper had a big argument about uniforms. The captain thought they would make us look more professional. Val thought it was an unnecessary expense. He doubled down, so she had that eyesore made as a joke. Only thing I've ever seen her spend money on. He dropped the issue, and he's never worn it, even on Halloween."

Ellis grinned. The *Violet Eel* had pulled out all the stops.

From where they stood at opposite ends of the line of tarps, Ilva and Connor could see Sebastian but not each other.

"Who is here to present this couple to the community and support them in their joining?" the captain asked, his theatricality emboldened by his ridiculous outfit.

Goosebumps rising on her arms, Ellis stepped forward. "I am," she replied in unison with Landon, who was at the other end of the tarps.

"Are you two prepared to join your lives?" Sebastian asked the happy couple. When they affirmed that they were, he nodded. "Then let the obstacles between you fall."

Ilva, looking elegant, struck a handheld drow gong. When she heard a matching noise from the other end of the room, she raised her arm, summoned a ball of shadow magic, and dissolved a hole in the first tarp. Normally, they would have been dissolving rock walls, but the tarps were an acceptable substitute, and Ilva and Connor proceeded toward each other. Ellis stepped through the hole behind Ilva as she rang the gong again. They did it twice more until a single tarp separated them.

"Let the fall of this final barrier be a symbol of your lasting love. You will be joined as a pair."

Ilva held her hand out again. Connor was standing on the other side of the tarp, so she worked more gingerly to take it down this time. Her magic twined with Connor's in the middle, and the last scraps of the tarp fell.

The crowd gathered around Ilva and Connor, who were staring at each other with a warmth Ellis had rarely seen in either. When the tarp fell, she saw Charlie for the first time since the start of the wedding. His face brightened when he saw her, and she returned his wave with a cheerful nod.

"You may now exchange rings," Sebastian stated. Ellis, who had managed to keep track of the band, produced it. The stone clinked against the black pearl on her forefinger, and she shivered. No one else seemed to notice, however, and the ceremony concluded with an exchange of rings and a thundering cheer. The tsunami of goodwill carried the wedding party up to the mess, where, in addition to the mushroom wine and the drow cake, Emily had put together a delicious spread and a two-tiered human wedding cake. All the formality had drained out of the party.

Charlie quickly appeared with two glasses of mushroom wine. "I never got invited to a wedding while I was at the Homestead. This was nice."

Ellis took one glass. She'd been too busy organizing the wedding to spend much time with Charlie. Or that had been her excuse. She'd found plenty of reasons to run into him, but those meetings had been just long enough for her to confirm that he was alive. "How are you doing?" she asked, sliding in beside him at one of the tables.

He reluctantly poked a sliver of mushroom cake. "I check my door a lot to make sure it opens. And I've been seasick."

"Did Jerel give you his magic potion?" Ellis asked. As an afterthought, she retrieved the bag of ginger chews, dumped half on the table, and slid them over. "And these should help."

"Rose wants off the boat. She has this idea about renting a house, or maybe borrowing one. I don't know the details. I want to go with her. Not sure a sailor's life is the life for me."

"Oh." Ellis' heart sank. She had to think of an excuse and fast. "We're safest here, with all the cloaking technology."

"Oh." Charlie looked disappointed. "Does that mean you won't come with me?"

Hope surged through her. "I didn't realize you were inviting me."

He slipped his hand across the table and grabbed hers but then jerked away. "Your ring is freezing." He rubbed a small white blister on his hand that had appeared when he touched it.

"I'm sorry." Ellis lowered her voice. "I haven't been able to take it off. I haven't told anyone else."

Resolutely, Charlie put his hand on hers, avoiding contact with the ring. "I'm sorry. How has it been?"

"The sword wants something, and I don't know what." Ellis took a swig of mushroom wine and immediately regretted it. What if the wine lowered her inhibitions so much that the sword took over? Charlie squeezed her hand, and she smiled. "If you leave, what will you do?"

"Try to rejoin the police force. Or if they won't have me, I suppose I'll get a job. You know I was a film projectionist one summer in college."

"I didn't know that."

"Plenty of work for projectionists in LA."

She couldn't imagine Charlie giving up police work. He liked getting into trouble too much. She took another sip of wine and put down the half-empty glass. Her phone alarm beeped, and Ellis looked at the time, startled.

"Fireworks!" she cried, climbing to her feet. "Help me herd people onto the deck?"

"Only if you come find me after," Charlie told her with a grin as he got to his feet. Ellis was by warmed his request.

Val had offered to do fireworks for the wedding. The *Violet Eel*'s explosives expert had spent days in the lab whipping up the right chemicals and loading them into tubes, and Val had taken a Zodiac to a safe distance from the ship to set them off. It was a peace offering to Ellis and the rest of the newcomers. When everyone was on the deck, Ellis found Charlie at the rail. He put an arm over her shoulder, and she snuggled into him. The sword and the ring made her cold, and she appreciated his body heat.

Ellis tapped her earpiece. "Val. We're ready."

It was a beautiful night for it, clear and starlit under a crescent moon. "Val…" she repeated. "Come in, Val."

There was no response. Ellis waited a full minute.

"Val?"

CHAPTER TWO

When the radio silence continued, Ellis went to find Ollie, the ship's comms officer. "I can't get Val."

His face told her that something was wrong, and they went to find Sebastian.

The captain was staring at the ocean through an old-fashioned pocket telescope. "I can't see her. She shouldn't have gone very far."

The ring on Ellis' finger twitched. "Something's wrong. Is it possible that someone attacked her?"

"They would have had to move fast," It wasn't a no. "Let's head to the navigation room and look at the radar."

The second they entered, Ellis knew they were in hot water. Every display was dead, the screens lifeless black squares. Sebastian stared blankly at his reflection in the nearest display, then picked up a yellow sticky note on the ship's wheel. He cursed under his breath as he read it.

"She disabled it," he growled.

"Disabled *what?*" Ollie asked incredulously.

"Everything," Sebastian shot back.

"*What?* What if there's a storm? Or pirates?" Ellis demanded.

"We're a stone's throw from multiple naval bases. And there are no *pirates.*" Ollie sounded too nervous to be condescending.

"What does the note say?" Ellis asked.

"She security-locked the engines. Claims everything will come back on in two hours." Sebastian crushed the note in his fist.

Ellis wished she could crush Val's head. "How far can she get in the Zodiac?"

"To shore, if she wants to go there," Sebastian said. "Pretty much any port between Ventura and San Diego."

He was still for a moment. He was so used to having Val as his right arm that his first instinct was to call for her. Instead, he paced for a few seconds before launching into action.

Sebastian sent a crew member to ring the emergency bell and hurried back onto the deck, screaming for attention. The clanging—the ship had an actual bell—got everyone on the deck focused as Ellis and Charlie waited nervously. When the crew and the wedding party had gathered, Sebastian told them he wanted a full inventory of the ship. They scattered in all directions. Ellis wished that she had a task to distract her too.

"What can I do?" Ellis asked after most of the crew had departed.

"Apologize to your father for me," Sebastian snarled as he headed toward the navigation room.

Ellis let him go. She was antsy, but she didn't know enough about the ship to be useful. She joined Connor and

Ilva at the rail. She had expected the pair to be angry, but they surprised her. Their arms twined comfortably on the salt-streaked rail, and they appeared unruffled by the chaos around them.

"I'm sorry," Ellis said. "So is Sebastian."

"I'm not." Connor favored Ilva with a rare smile. Landon wandered over, and a small, ungracious part of Ellis flared with envy as his parents embraced him and each other. It was not that she had wanted Connor to remarry Claire, but Landon's family unit was whole in a way Ellis' could never be. She pushed the feeling away and joined them.

"Our relationship has never been boring," Ilva glanced at Ellis. "Why should our wedding be any different?"

"I wanted to see the fireworks," Landon whined. He loved explosions.

"At least it's a nice night," Ellis chirped.

Rose came over to ask if they'd seen Percy. "Sebastian asked me to find him." Ellis offered to help her look. Percy was usually on deck so he could chat with passing birds. They found Percy on the bow, head dangling off the deck.

"Percy…" Ellis began. He didn't answer, although Mariner the albatross, who was perched on a nearby lifeboat, squawked.

"Percy, love," Rose called. Percy's silver head whipped around, and he grinned.

"I met a whale!" He sounded giddy as he pulled himself up to a sitting position.

"Really? What kind?" Rose asked, grasping the rail and peering into the dark water below.

"A fin whale. Fast little bugger. They can swim as fast as a battleship if they want."

Rose looked apologetic. "I hate to pull you away from a new friend, but Sebastian needs you belowdecks."

"What's wrong?" Percy asked.

Why would Sebastian need Percy? There weren't many animals aboard the *Eel*. The ship had a black and white tuxedo cat as a good luck charm, but it was fat and well-fed and mostly stayed in the lounge. Vermin in the hold, maybe? If so, Sebastian was barking up the wrong tree. "If he's having rat problems, Percy won't be able to help," Ellis told her.

"I could help the rats," Percy pointed out.

"Like I said," Ellis grumbled. She announced that she was going with them and headed back to the navigation room. Rose stopped her. "I'm supposed to take him belowdecks."

Ellis glanced down and realized they were going toward the Violet Eye, the ship's powerful computer system.

"That's not good," Ellis whispered.

While she'd been talking to Rose, Percy had resumed his conversation with the whale. It took both their efforts to pull him away.

"Tell the whale we're not going anywhere for a few hours," Ellis muttered. "You can chat later." She explained to Percy that Val had disabled the navigation systems. He'd been too absorbed in his conversation with the whale to notice the chaos.

As they approached the room housing the Violet Eye, the corridors were chaotic. They were less than halfway down the hall when Sebastian strode up and grabbed Percy's arm.

"What's going on?" Ellis asked. Sebastian ignored her and pulled Percy through the door into the server room. Ellis trotted down the narrow aisle behind them. The system appeared to be running, lights blinking and water running through the cooling tubes.

Percy, who was not a big fan of being manhandled, sidled out of Sebastian's grip with a yelp of dismay. "More information and less prodding, please," he mumbled.

Sebastian waved the request away. "You're a hacker. I need you to tell me what's going on." He pushed Percy into the swivel chair in front of the Violet Eye's workstation.

"I can't tell you what's going on if you don't return the favor," Percy replied evenly, although he took the seat. Then he froze with a far-off look in his eyes.

"What is it?" Sebastian asked.

Percy was unresponsive, mind elsewhere. After a moment, he shook his head. "Just saying a few goodbyes."

"He met a whale," Ellis explained.

Sebastian looked unconvinced. The past few days had been too much of a whirlwind for him to embrace the existence of an animal psychic, even though the ship's cat liked Percy, and the crew now included an albatross that exhibited uncanny behavior.

"It's fine. We made plans to meet up later." Percy smiled.

Sebastian's eyes were bright, and the purple freckles dotting his face were dark. "Val took something from the Eye, and I need to know what."

Percy opened a window on the computer, and his fingers flew across the keyboard. When it asked him for a password, he paused. "You'd be better off with someone who knows the system."

"I would be," Sebastian agreed through gritted teeth. "Unfortunately, Meryn went with Val."

"He's your top dog?" Percy asked.

"He created the Violet Eye," Sebastian snarled. "I can't believe he would destroy it like this."

"Well, maybe he didn't. I need admin credentials." Percy tapped the screen.

Sebastian was quiet.

"Let me guess." Percy sighed. "Meryn's the only one who can hand out credentials."

"He's loyal," Sebastian protested. "I was the best man at his first and third weddings."

Percy's eyebrow climbed.

Desperation made Sebastian's voice sound hollow. "Can you tell me *anything?*"

"What did she actually take?" Percy looked around. He tapped the screen and glanced at the servers. "I mean, what might she have been after? Passwords for offshore accounts? Real estate titles? Would she, say, sell intelligence to a foreign government?"

Sebastian's freckles went fire-engine red. "Val's not a traitor. She wouldn't sell us out for a payday."

"You sure about that?" Percy swung the chair back and forth with an irritating squeak.

"That's the *only* thing I'm sure of right now. Val never took vacations. She barely touched her salary, although a few times, I caught her spending her own money on supplies for the ship."

"What about the suit?" Ellis asked, grinning. Sebastian

had taken off the tricorn hat but was still wearing the purple suit. It didn't diminish his authority.

Ellis tapped Percy's chair, thinking the problem through. "Let's say I take you at your word. If Val didn't care about money, what *did* she care about?"

"The *Violet Eel* and its mission. And me, although…" His voice trailed off, and he frowned.

"Trouble in paradise?" Ellis asked lightly.

"She was furious when I told her what happened in the silo," Sebastian admitted.

"You mean that you held my friends captive in an attempt to take my sword and forced Rami to lose an arm in the process?"

Sebastian winced but nodded. "Yes. It got worse when I told her that we agreed I'd wait a month before making a decision about revealing the drow's existence to the world."

"She felt betrayed." Ellis nodded. "Which might make someone who values loyalty above all else very dangerous."

"I guess so." Sebastian sighed. "So, you think she wanted revenge?"

"That's one explanation." Percy tapped the keyboard without typing, lost in thought.

Sebastian crossed his arms and stared at Percy. "Can you help me or not? I need a hacker, not a psychologist."

"I'm not so sure about that." Percy spun to face the captain. He made a full circuit with the chair, and this time, even Ellis felt nervy. After a moment, he went back to typing. "None of the servers are gone or stripped, so unless this was sabotage, in which case my presence is moot, she transferred the data she took to external storage.

She didn't have that long to work. Do you have a thumb drive?"

Ellis and Sebastian fished in their pockets, and Sebastian produced a small blue rectangle.

"I thought you didn't have access?" Sebastian queried.

"I'm just testing the data transfer rate," Percy explained. "Give me a minute." Sebastian paced the aisles, and Ellis sank onto the deck, leaning back against the only bulkhead not crammed with tech equipment. After a few minutes, he called Sebastian back.

"You know what she took?" Sebastian asked eagerly.

Percy shook his head. "No, but based on the data transfer rate and her login/logoff times, I know approximately how much data she took. Pretty much a dead match with a file called 'Operation Omni.' Doesn't mean anything to me, but I'm guessing you might have an idea."

Although it seemed impossible, Sebastian's freckles got darker. Maybe it was just that the skin around them turned paler.

"What is it?" Ellis demanded.

Sebastian shook his head. "That's the database with the location of every drow homestead we know about. Even..."

"What?" Ellis grabbed Sebastian's collar.

"Even the ones that wanted nothing to do with us. Drow communities with no interest in making contact with humans."

"You said it was up to them if they wanted to join your program," Ellis protested.

"It was! Or it was supposed to be," Sebastian stated uncertainly.

"We have to assume that Val has new plans," Ellis mused.

"She didn't betray us," Sebastian shot back. "Not in her mind, anyway. She's moving forward with our original plan."

"What plan?" Percy asked.

Ellis hesitated. She'd only told two humans the location of the drow Homestead. One was Charlie, and the other was her mother. Charlie's visit to the Homestead had turned out poorly, and Claire's had been a disaster. But Ellis trusted Percy, and if Val was about to spill the beans, he deserved to know the full story. "You know the drow."

"Purple skin? Midnight vibes?" Percy grinned.

"Yeah, those are the ones. Anyway, I'm sure you've realized that we have a homestead. It's a cave system under the Angeles National Forest. So far, we've kept the location secret. About ten thousand of us live there."

Percy whistled. "That's more than I thought."

"Yeah, well, if the US military drops a nuke on them, there might not be any soon." Ellis glared at Sebastian.

"We still don't know what Val's planning," Sebastian countered.

"What, exactly, do you think she's doing? Saving all the addresses so she can send the drow *Violet Eel* gift baskets?"

"Probably not," the captain agreed.

"What was the plan? Give us as many details as you can so we can figure out what she is doing."

"We had a vanguard of drow communities in Canada, France, and Japan who were going to come out. Countries with powerful allies but small militaries. The *Violet Eel* would send drow ambassadors with small magical gifts—

healing potions and that kind of thing—and we'd release a burst of PR materials showing everyday life in drow communities."

"Smiling kids? Traditional crafts?" Percy asked.

"Exactly."

"Are the people who were assigned to be ambassadors still on the ship?" Ellis asked.

"Yes," Sebastian grumbled. "That's what's so frustrating. There's no way she can execute the plan by herself."

Percy's chair squeaked as he swung back and forth until Sebastian lost his cool and shouted at him to stop. When Percy got to his feet, Sebastian apologized.

Percy shrugged. "I'm a fidgety guy. If you want, I can brute-force your system, but that might take a hot minute."

"How hot?" Sebastian asked.

"Like, weeks," Percy admitted.

Sebastian pressed his fingertips to his forehead. "No. Whatever Val's up to, it'll be over by then."

Percy nodded and scooted down the aisle toward the hatch. "If that was all you needed?"

"Yeah. That was all. Go talk to your whale."

Percy was gone before Sebastian looked up. He and Ellis were now alone. He stared at the tip of the void scabbard peeking over her shoulder with regret in his eyes.

"Well, what do we do now?" Ellis asked.

As he was about to answer, his watch beeped.

"Captain? This is Ollie."

"This better be an emergency."

"And then some." Ollie sounded agitated. "We've got a Navy cruiser incoming."

"Shit!" Sebastian left the server room at a run.

Not wanting to be useless, Ellis trailed after Sebastian, although there wasn't much she could do about an incoming battleship.

You could slice it in half, a small voice told her. A chill shot into her back from the void sword's scabbard. Ellis tried to laugh the thought away, but a current shot down her spine.

"Stop," she muttered to the sword. She continued onto the deck and ran up to a stocky young drow crewmember with an ice-blue mohawk. "What's going on?"

"Absolutely fucking nothing," the sailor replied. "The engines are down, so we can't move, and we can't turn on the ship's invisibility envelope. I'd say we were sitting ducks, but ducks can generally fly away."

The woman excused herself to go be angry at someone in her chain of command. Sebastian, visible in one of the navigation room's windows, was in conference with his officers. They wouldn't need or want her opinions, or not when it came to boats, so she went to the top deck, where the helicopter pad sat empty.

There was a squawk from the rail. Ellis looked over to see Mariner perched on the whitewashed metal. "You can't fight off a battleship, can you?"

Mariner squawked again, puffed out her feathers, preened, and shook. Ellis took that as a no. "Fine. Don't help us, then." As if in response, the ship's bell rang again. Ellis made her way back down to the main deck, where the crew was assembling.

Ollie was face-to-face with the captain, their mood just below violence. "You must have known something was happening. You were behind this."

"I was *not*." Sebastian looked to his right, expecting Val to appear at his side. Ollie noted the gesture and shoved the captain.

"If you can't even keep a handle on Val, you don't deserve to captain this ship." Ollie's hands went out to his sides as if he expected physical retaliation.

"Do you want to start a fight, or do you want to deal with the existing situation as a crew?" Sebastian asked. "I'm sure that battleship has a comfortable brig for us to cool off in."

Ollie grunted in disgust and crossed his arms.

"Thank you." Sebastian gave a small smile. "You're lucky I need you at your station, or you'd be in *our* brig. Look, we will raise our merchant flag. If you're human or human-passing, stay at your station. Everyone else hides in the server room. Now, people!"

The crew ran in all directions, and Ellis went to find her family. A young crewmember was leading them belowdecks.

Not knowing where else to go, Ellis followed Sebastian to the navigation room. He delivered orders to a small group of officers as she tucked herself into the corner. The plan, apparently, was to pretend to be a Swedish merchant ship. The story was that they were having engine trouble and had veered off their normal route for repairs.

Ellis, who guessed the Navy would see that they were well-armed, was dubious that the plan would work. Unable to sit still any longer, she begged Sebastian's telescope off him and went back up to the helicopter pad.

She was the first person to see the cluster of boats on the horizon. At first, they were just dots, even with the telescope. Soon, Ellis could make out individual shapes, first of the vessels and then their weapons, motoring out from the naval cruiser as an attack force.

The small, hard-shelled boats were equipped with fifty-caliber machine guns and M-29 mortars. Their merchant flag looked suddenly thin and shabby. Ellis found Sebastian on the main deck, standing at the rail. He had changed into his usual garb, but he still seemed uncomfortable.

"Captain!" Ellis handed him his telescope. "I've been watching the Navy boats approach. I don't think they're coming to fix the engines."

"What makes you say that?"

"Have you ever fixed an engine with an M-29 mortar?"

Sebastian frowned and shook his head. "Maybe they're just being cautious."

"I don't know. Do you think Val turned us in?"

He shook his head so fiercely that his hat slid sideways. "No. Truly, no."

"If they know what we did at the silo, this is going to get ugly," Ellis cautioned.

"Maybe don't wave the magic sword around." Sebastian stared at where it poked up above her shoulder.

Ellis made sure her cloaker and the hush puppy were in her pocket and went down to the science lab to retrieve another bottle of the shadow magic potion. It took her a moment of searching the fridges to find the bottles lined up in a row on a bottom shelf. Fortunately, they were labeled.

As Ellis grabbed a full bottle, the faint rat-a-tat-tat of gunfire was audible through the deck. Cursing under her breath, Ellis grabbed a second bottle, drained the dregs of her old one, and chucked the empty in the trash on the way out. Shadows surged around her, and an icy blast of energy radiated from the sword on her back.

Securing the potion bottles in a waist pack, Ellis headed up to the main deck. When she saw starlight through the window on the swinging door, she flicked on the cloaker and hush puppy, then slipped outside slowly so she wouldn't arouse suspicions.

A khaki-clad sailor was holding Sebastian at gunpoint, and more were fanning out along the rails. Ellis sidestepped two of them as she crept closer to hear what Sebastian was saying. "Just take a look at our paperwork."

"Must be some pretty fancy paperwork to explain why a merchant vessel is armed with torpedo tubes."

Sebastian, who was a lot more nervous than an actual merchant captain would be, explained, "They were there when we refitted the boat. We use them for storage."

Sebastian was quick on his feet, but the sailor looked unconvinced. "My crew will take over operations." He jerked his gun to indicate the aluminum ladder the men had used to board the ship. "You'll be plenty warm and cozy in our brig."

The sailor led Sebastian to the rail, and Ellis crept behind them.

"No funny business or the man behind you will shoot you." The sailor pushed Sebastian onto the ladder. An armed man supervised his descent.

I have to help him. Invisibility only went so far in close quarters. The deck was crowded, and her opponent was well-armed. A hard-shelled boat was waiting below, manned by a single sailor. There were only two ways to get to Sebastian: she could go down the ladder, or she could try to make her way into the boat from the water. Ellis wished she had her grappling gun, but she would have to make do. *Ladder it is.* Making a split-second decision, she vaulted up and over the rail.

The aluminum ladder shook when she landed, twisting in the air like a double helix. One of the sailors shouted a confused warning, although Ellis was invisible, and Sebastian clearly hadn't done anything. Sebastian glanced suspiciously above him but was careful not to stare too long.

The naval launch bobbed, its distracted helmsman making continuous adjustments to keep it alongside the *Eel*. Finally, Sebastian dropped onto the hard deck. The aluminum rungs shook as another sailor began climbing down the ladder—Sebastian's escort.

Ellis descended more quickly. When she was ten feet above the boat, she watched the helmsman work. If she missed her jump, she would go into the ocean again, and she didn't have a life jacket this time. Adjusting to the way the ladder swung as the sailor above her climbed down, she braced her feet against the rough hull of the boat and leapt, intending to drop onto the helmsman like a flying squirrel.

Instead, she hit the gunwale with her stomach. The hush puppy suppressed her cry of pain as the hard corner punched the air out of her stomach, but the boat dipped violently in the water, and a cold swell washed over her, freezing where it touched the black scabbard on her back.

The sword wanted to be drawn. It sang out for violence on a psychic channel, but Ellis ignored it since the helmsman had left his post and was coming to find out why the port side of his boat was dipping into the water.

Because there are too many people on this goddamn dinghy. Ellis forced herself upright, straddling the side of the boat. The second the sailor came into the envelope of her cloaker, she grabbed the front of his life vest and flung him into the ocean as far as she could.

"Hello?" Sebastian asked, peering at the invisible form. Ellis didn't turn off her cloaker.

There was a shout from above. The sailor at the railing swiveled his gun and aimed down the side of the boat, but the angle made it a struggle, and he was unwilling to fire blindly into the dark water his brother-in-arms was swimming in.

Ellis dove for the wheel. Her plan had been to steer away from the ship, but that would allow the sailors lining the *Violet Eel*'s rail to fire at the boat. She reached for the pack at her waist, retrieved a bottle of potion, and chugged half of it.

Shadow magic roared up around her, lapping at her skin, and Ellis concentrated. The ocean contained a fair amount of shadow magic on the surface at night. Underneath, there was a nearly infinite well of power rising up from the fathoms light never touched. Ellis reached for this glut of swirling purple and pulled it up like she was raising an anchor, then spun it into sheets that she draped over the hard-shelled attack boat.

"Where the fuck did the boat go?" someone shouted from up top, and Ellis cheered. She had done it. She had cloaked them. She spun the wheel, and the boat jerked out into the ocean. As they bounced across the waves, she focused. She couldn't keep the boat invisible for long and wanted to gain some distance.

The helmsman she'd thrown overboard was floundering in the water at the bottom of the ladder. He had swum over and was trying to haul himself onto the lowest rung, which was near the surface as it bobbed in and out of the waves.

Ellis flicked off the hush puppy. "We have to get out of here."

"Ellis." Sebastian looked conflicted. "Thanks for coming to get me, but we have to go back."

"I know. I'm going to get back on board and get everyone off, but I need you here."

"I won't abandon my ship."

"A ship is just a big house floating on the water. The important thing is the crew, and the crew needs you. How many people can we get on the Zodiacs?"

"Not many. Less than half. There's plenty of room in the lifeboats, but they don't have propulsion. We'd be as vulnerable as we are on the *Eel*. Maybe more."

"Shit. Well, we'll just have to figure it out."

Seb stayed quiet, freckled face stony in the moonlight.

Ellis looked toward the ship. "You're better at steering than I am. Take me back to the ladder."

"What? That's crazy. There are guns everywhere."

"I know. I'm going to stay invisible."

"No one's that good at shadow magic," Sebastian countered.

"I am." Ellis hoped it was true. Sebastian shook his head but changed places with her. Soon, they were heading back to the ship.

"I can't keep the boat invisible," Sebastian told Ellis as they neared the dangling end of the ladder.

"I know. Do you still have your cloaker?"

"No. I ditched it before I gave myself up. I didn't want the Navy to confiscate our shadow magic technology."

"That *would* open up a can of worms." Ellis reluctantly handed Sebastian her cloaker. If her shadow magic reserves got drained or she lost her potions, she'd be in trouble, but he needed it more than she did. They would just have to risk it.

"Are you sure?" Sebastian asked.

"I can get by on potion when I go back up. I'll keep you and the boat invisible as long as I can, but eventually, it'll look like this thing is empty. Let it bounce against the ship. That'll confuse them if nothing else."

Sebastian nodded and steered toward the ladder, saluting as she hauled herself onto the lower rungs. She wrapped another sheet of shadow magic around the boat as she got her balance. "Okay. Go."

Sebastian turned the wheel, and the boat moved away. Ellis concentrated, sending out wave after wave of concealing magic. Soon, it thinned. When Sebastian was a few dozen feet away, the shadow magic reached its limit and snapped. The boat looked empty, and there were confused shouts from the deck. It offered a nice distraction as Ellis ascended the ladder.

The sailor in charge of the mission was arguing with his second in command when Ellis reached the deck. The gist of the argument was that half the crew seemed to have disappeared. Ellis grinned, although the cloakers would make it hard for her to round everyone up and get them off the ship.

Shadow-magic-detecting goggles would let her see

anyone using a cloaker. Ellis considered where the nearest pair might be and decided her best bet was the nav room. The Navy had turned it into a temporary detention center, stuffing it full of the *Violet Eel*'s human crew members, which meant that the door was guarded. Ellis walked the room's perimeter, peering through the windows. There wasn't much cover, but there was a spot near the back that was out of sight of the guards where she might be able to get through. Still, the odds were bad.

A shrill squawk diverted Ellis' attention, followed by the clicks of nails. She looked up to see Mariner on the roof of the nav room. Inspiration dawning, Ellis swung up to join the massive albatross. Although she was invisible, the bird looked in her direction, alerted by vibrations in the metal deck. Or maybe Mariner was one of those animals with a sixth sense for shadow magic.

Drawing the void sword, Ellis found a spot near the center of the nav room. After checking to make sure no one was watching, she plunged the blade into the deck at her feet and drew it in a manhole-sized circle. The void sword sliced through the roof like it was plastic. Ellis grabbed the circle of metal before it fell, slid it sideways, and hopped through the hole. She landed on top of the table in the middle of the room.

Several crew members had seen a new skylight appear but were wise enough not to raise an alarm. Ellis flicked off her hush puppy for a second. "It's me," she whispered.

Ollie jumped, and one of the guards looked over.

"Play it cool," Ellis whispered. He took a deep breath and nodded. "I'm here to get everyone off the ship, but I need a pair of shadow magic goggles. Is there one in here?"

"Mmhm," Ollie whispered back. "Port bulkhead."

Ellis nodded. "Good. Give me a second." She wound her way in that direction. When she arrived, she collected the goggles from a hook. "Okay. Got 'em."

"What's your plan?" Ollie asked. The guards outside seemed uninterested in their captives. Their attention was focused on the deck.

"I'm winging it," Ellis admitted. "I don't think we can storm the deck, and climbing onto the roof will leave us exposed. What's below us?"

"Mess."

"Okay, that's where we're going. I'll cut a big hole in the floor, and everyone will jump. Do you still have your cloakers?"

"Enough to cover us," Ollie replied. "Some of us will have to pair up."

"Do it. No big moves."

The bodies around her shifted. Ellis directed, "Everyone move toward the walls, but try not to make it obvious." Nodding, the crew moseyed toward the portholes a few at a time. "I'm going to cut through to the mess hall. Once you're down there, get out fast and make your way back on the deck. There's a hard-shelled inflatable boat off the bow that as many of you as can fit need to get to. That's where Sebastian is. The rest of you will have to go in the lifeboats."

"The lifeboats don't have propulsion," Ollie protested. "They're just big rubber rafts."

"You can stay here and enjoy military detention if you prefer. I'll do my best to get everyone out free and clear."

Several people nodded. Ellis had to trust that they understood.

Ellis unsheathed the void sword and sliced through the deck. Unlike the overhead, this was a thick layer of metal and wood. The black blade went through it like it was air, vibrating with enthusiasm. *"Now!"*

She finished the cut and leapt on the center of the disc, riding it down as it slammed into the tables below. When the dust settled, *Violet Eel* crewmembers poured down around her, helping each other out of the rubble and popping out of view as their cloakers activated.

Ellis donned the pilfered shadow magic goggles to make sure everyone got out. She heard shouts from above, but fortunately, no gunfire. When she was sure everyone had made it out, Ellis raced out of the mess toward the server room. She was tense, and every time she turned a corner, she was afraid of walking into gunfire, but she encountered no one before she reached the secret hatch to the server farm.

Ellis pressed the sequence of rivets that released the lock and flung the hatch open the instant it appeared. When she barged in, she found herself staring at the obsidian point of a drow arrow.

"Oh." Ilva lowered her bow and slipped the arrow back into its quiver.

Her father hugged her. "What's going on?"

Ellis didn't respond since there was noise in the passage. As she peered out the hatch, several well-armed sailors descended the ladder at the end of the passage. One of them spotted her, and time seemed to slow as he pulled the trigger of his weapon. Ellis instinctively raised the void sword in front of her and watched with alarm as bullets approached and hit the broad side of the blade. The sword vibrated, and the bullets disappeared, sucked into the void.

She gaped but slipped back into the server farm, then slammed the hatch shut and activated the lock. A few minutes later, gunshots rang out, and dents appeared in the hatch. It held, but it wouldn't do so forever.

"We're trapped," Connor remarked.

"No. We're not." Ellis raised her sword. "If someone tries to stop us, I will cut them down."

She considered the ship's layout. They needed enough life jackets for the whole crew, especially the drow who couldn't swim. That meant they needed to return to the main deck. Even if they fought off the men at the hatch, they would face several decks of opposition.

The hatch rattled as something heavier than bullets pounded it. Ellis guessed they had less than five minutes before the metal failed.

"Boost me up." Ellis pointed at the nearest server tower. Powered by the ship's emergency generators, green and red lights twinkled at her. Her father hoisted Ellis up. After she found her footing amid the cooling tubes, she raised the void sword again.

A frisson of pleasure rushed through her as the blade bit into the metal. The sword sang, and Ellis' soul sang with it. It didn't slice through the overhead so much as consume it, destroying the matter the blade touched. Ellis was feeding the sword, and the sword was feeding her in turn. Electrical wires sparked, but the blade absorbed the charge. Soon, light streamed in from above.

The newly cut passage led into an unfamiliar crew

cabin. Ellis glanced around, then went inside and pulled the others through. Climbing was harder than jumping down, and it took a few minutes to escort the group up into the new space. They took turns casting invisibility and muffling spells as they clambered into the cabin. As a stray elbow took her in the guts, Ellis saw a motivational poster one of the crew members had plastered to the bulkhead. Under a glistening, muscular man lifting a barbell, it said, *PAIN IS WEAKNESS LEAVING THE BODY.*

Another elbow relieved Ellis of a little more weakness, and she grunted. They had to get off this ship and soon.

Sailors with guns patrolled the passage outside the crew quarters, but they hadn't been alerted to the possibility of someone coming up through the deck. The space got cramped as more drow from the server room flooded in and scrunched onto the racks.

"I'm going to go get us life jackets," Ellis stated. "Stay here, and stay invisible. Be ready when I get back." The invisible crowd murmured in assent. Maneuvering toward the hatch, she watched a sailor patrol the passage, waiting until he was just outside. Then she dispelled her invisibility spell with a flick of her fingers and waved through the warped plastic porthole. The sailor jerked so hard his body armor rattled, and Ellis swung the hatch out and slammed it against the guard's torso. He flew into the opposite bulkhead.

She gripped the sword hilt and sliced down the barrel of the fallen sailor's rifle, cutting it nearly in half. Then she took off toward the nearest ladder, ignoring the hair-raising feeling of being exposed. She clutched a juicy ball of shadow magic in her left hand, but she had to draw the guards off and couldn't afford to start a manhunt so close to where the drow were hiding.

She stayed visible until she reached the top of the ladder, then slowed and allowed the sailor she'd knocked down to catch up.

If she unexpectedly burst onto the deck, she would draw gunfire, so she waited until the last moment. As the guard's fingers brushed her shirt, she flung the hatch open and out onto the deck, simultaneously wrapping herself in an invisibility spell.

The guard's mad stumble after the empty space where she'd been disguised her exit, and she pulled herself out of the fray onto the top of a nearby storage crate while he stumbled around on the waxed wood. Barely pausing to breathe, she searched the deck.

Large numbers of life jackets were stored under the benches that ran along the sides of the ship. Getting to them was the problem. Each side was patrolled by a sailor with a rifle.

Stealth alone wouldn't cut it. Ellis needed a distraction, and after watching the sailors patrol for a few minutes, Ellis made her move. Creeping along the starboard rail, Ellis fell into step behind the guard, then dove forward and chucked him over the rail.

As the sailors on deck ran toward the sounds of his screams, Ellis moved to the other side of the boat and threw open the nearest storage bench's lid. In addition to a profusion of orange life jackets, she found a length of blue rope and strung it through the vests' armholes. That created a puffy tangerine-colored lei, and she dropped it over her head.

Welcome to Hawaii! As an afterthought, she tossed the last life vest in the box overboard. Hopefully, it would be of use to the sailor she'd thrown over.

When she turned back, however, there was a new problem. Uniformed men had established a perimeter around the hatch from which she'd emerged. She could not get to the opening without going through them, and she was reluctant to use more violence. She had only used ten or so feet of rope for the life jackets, and she freed the rest of the coil. More than what she needed, she thought. Running to the nearest rail, Ellis looped the rope around it, tied it off with a figure-eight, and flung the loose coil overboard. It whipped down to the water. Grabbing it with one hand, she hopped over, planted her feet against the hull, and rappelled down to the portholes of the crew cabins.

These were just above the water, and she peered inside as she traversed the hull to find the right cabin. Finally, she spotted the motivational poster featuring the grimacing weightlifter. Rearranging her life jacket lei, she pulled the void sword out of its scabbard and donned the shadow magic goggles. Swirling purple bubbles indicated either invisibility spells or cloakers in the room. Selecting her spot carefully, Ellis cut a small hole in one porthole.

"Hey!" Ellis whispered through it. "It's me."

"Ellis?" Ilva asked. "How did you get… You know what? Never mind."

"Get everyone away from the window," Ellis ordered. Working carefully, she cut a large hole in the hull of the ship. After shoving the life jackets through, she hopped inside.

One at a time, the group donned orange life jackets and

jumped into the water. Fortunately, the cloakers were designed to hold up under anything short of a nuclear bomb, so the group would stay invisible. Also, at this time of night, the drow had plenty of shadow magic available. The drow were fairly resistant to hypothermia, but it would be difficult for the human crew to be immersed for long.

Ellis checked Trissa's life jacket and helped her climb through the enlarged porthole. "There will be lifeboats in the water soon. I promise." Trissa's face was pale, but she nodded and leapt into the dark water with a splash. Landon followed her.

A deckhand with dark blue skin stepped up. "You'll need more than a lifeboat to save you after Captain Seb finds out you cut a hole in his ship," he muttered as he took Ellis' hand, staring nervously at the dark horizon.

Ilva laid a hand on Ellis' shoulder. The crowd had thinned out, but she hadn't seen her father. She had a sinking feeling. *That's what you get when you cut a bunch of holes in the side of a boat. A sinking feeling.*

"Where's Dad?" Ellis demanded when she realized that Ilva was the last person in the room.

Ilva's face was troubled. "Landon wanted to go to the brig. He said he didn't want to let any drow fall into the Navy's custody."

Ellis' face reddened. "Admirable, but stupid."

"A family trait," Ilva stated.

"He didn't go, though," Ellis looked out the open porthole. Her brother was in the water.

"Landon agreed to stay here when Connor said he would go instead."

Ellis' heart sank. Her father and Landon had both been imprisoned and experimented on by the DRI, and they didn't want anyone else to go through that. Of course they didn't trust the military. She was ashamed that *she* hadn't thought about Mirelle.

The Russians the drow had pulled off Marusya Klimova's yacht had been extradited to their home country, but few would face charges. It wasn't perfect justice, but Sebastian said it was the best they could do. Only Mirelle was left in the *Violet Eel*'s brig, trapped in a limbo no one had puzzled a way out of.

Ellis understood why Connor had gone, but she wished he hadn't gone alone. "You go ahead. I'll go get Dad."

"Thank you." Ilva buckled the life jacket around her waist and adjusted the straps. "I'd hate to see our marriage be this short-lived."

A swell crashed into the side of the *Eel*, soaking both of them and running across the floor in rivulets. The sky had darkened, and after a second wave hit the boat, Ellis realized that clouds had blocked the stars.

"Be safe," Ellis called as Ilva dove into the water.

CHAPTER THREE

Brandishing the void sword, Ellis kicked her way out into the passage and went to the brig, searching cabins for drow who had stayed hidden as she went. She saw no one until she reached the hatch to a narrow ladder. Just beside it, tucked into the corner, was a shadow magic bubble. Ellis slipped inside the invisibility envelope.

"Hi, Dad," Ellis greeted.

"You should have evacuated," he told her sternly, although he looked relieved to see her.

"So should you. What's the situation?"

The Navy had secured the brig during their initial search, which meant they had found Mirelle. Because she was in a lightsilk-treated cell where she couldn't use shadow magic, she hadn't been able to turn invisible. Predictable chaos had ensued, and the brig was heavily guarded. The atmosphere bristled with both guns and anxiety.

Ellis handed her father a life jacket. "Put this on." He

complied without protest, and she did the same. Then she drew her sword.

Connor stared at the dark blade, which seemed to absorb the light.

"I've been thinking," Ellis commented.

Connor grunted. "A dangerous pastime."

"We need to get everyone off the ship, and we can't let the Navy have it. Not any of it, particularly the servers." Connor understood better than anyone what the military could do with shadow magic technology and a list of drow homesteads. "I didn't just come here to keep Mirelle and the others from falling into the Navy's hands. I came to keep *everything* from falling into the Navy's hands, from the crew to the server room to the goggles on my head."

"You have a plan?"

Ellis hesitated. It wasn't a good plan, but it was all she had. "I'm going to sink the ship," she announced, her face hard.

Her father looked more curious than alarmed. "How?"

"I'm going to cut it to pieces. If the ship starts sinking, they'll have to take Mirelle out of the brig."

"Will they?" Connor asked. He had a dim view of the military's ethics.

"They'll either evacuate her or abandon her. We can take advantage of the chaos."

The void sword vibrated eagerly, and Ellis squeezed the hilt. She was about to offer it a feast, and it was ready. She and her father descended to the level below the brig. Ellis didn't know much about ship construction. Where would a hole in the hull do the most damage?

I'll poke it until I find out. Not wanting to overthink things, Ellis went to the side of an auxiliary cargo hold and told her father to stand back. The sword twitched toward its quarry, and Ellis stabbed the hull at random. The sword slid through the metal but juddered when it hit the pressurized water below. She sensed that the sword was sucking up great quantities of saltwater. As Ellis removed the blade, there was a horrible creak and a hiss, and saltwater sprayed into the room. Ellis stabbed again, and another stream jetted into the hold.

"Is that your plan?" Connor asked.

Ellis shrugged. "I'll stab the ship until my knees are wet. Let's go do the other side."

They moved across the hold, and she thrust the sword into the hull. The ocean streamed through the holes she cut, and the bulkhead turned into a fountain reminiscent of the Bellagio in Las Vegas. Warping under the pressure, the bulkhead shrieked. A moment later, she and her father were standing in knee-high water.

"Time to move up a level," she announced. As they went to the hatch, she saw movement in the passage. A team of sailors had come down to check out the problem. Wrapped in invisibility spells, Ellis and Connor carefully avoided them. Ellis grinned at their confused interchanges.

"What the fuck is doing this, a shark with a lightsaber?" one lieutenant asked. His buddy was too scared to reply, and they both moved toward the hold Ellis and Connor had just vacated.

The chaos around the brig evaporated as the Navy evacuated the ship, but two guards stood by the cell door, having a nervous tete-a-tete. There was apparently some debate about whether and how to evacuate Mirelle.

The lightsilk on the *Violet Eel* wasn't like the fabric the DRI used. It was gentler, and it didn't cause pain. Ellis was unsure of how quickly Mirelle's shadow magic would return after she was released, and she wasn't thrilled by the idea of the young drow dissolving the sailors' heads, but she couldn't warn them away.

One of the sailors was arguing that Mirelle's skin was purple because of radiation poisoning or worse, an exotic new illness. She might be contagious. The other sailor insisted she was a genetically engineered super soldier. They both wanted to wait for orders from their higher-ups, but the water was thigh-high and rising.

That turned out to be the deciding factor. When the sailors finally decided to release Mirelle, they found that the water pressure was so high that the hatch wouldn't budge. The sailor tugged once, twice, and gave up with a shrug.

"Fuck it. I'm outta here." He headed toward Connor and Ellis, and they pulled back into a small alcove as the man reached the ladder and hauled himself up and out of the water. The other sailor stared nervously at the cell door, then followed his brother-in-arms. When they were gone, Ellis and Connor slogged through the waist-high water to the cell. They peered through the small, transparent slit in the door, and Ellis dispersed her invisibility spell.

Mirelle jumped when Ellis' face appeared. She leapt to her feet and pounded on the door. "Get me out!" Water was streaming under the gap at the bottom of the door, and more was flowing in through gaps in the corners.

Ellis searched the brig, which held a desk and a few chairs and an unplugged microwave. There was a row of hooks along the far bulkhead, from which hung a nightstick and—Ellis perked up—two pairs of handcuffs. A plan formed in her mind. If she sliced a hole in the door, Mirelle would come out, dissolve her head and Connor's head, leave the brig, and wreak havoc. But one pair of handcuffs was padded with lightsilk.

Ellis reached out with the void sword and sliced a hole in the cell door at chest-level, which was just above the water.

"What are you doing?" Mirelle demanded. "It's not big enough. I can't get through."

Ellis picked up the cuffs, careful not to touch the padding. "Put your hands out."

"What? No! There's no time."

"Give me your wrists, and I'll let you out," Ellis repeated. "Or don't, and drown." For a horrible moment, she thought Mirelle might call her bluff, but the woman pounded on the door for another minute, then grudgingly slid her hands through the hole. Ellis secured the cuffs around Mirelle's wrists and told her to stand back. The void sword sliced through water and metal and created a large arched hole in the door.

As Mirelle stepped through, buckling metal screeched at the end of the passage. With a final creak, a torrent of water blasted into the brig. They could not get up the stairs.

Mirelle tried to wriggle out of the cuffs. "What are we going to do?"

"We're going to have to swim out," Ellis stated.

"I can't swim!" Mirelle protested.

"Neither can I. The life jackets will do most of the work."

"I don't have a life jacket," Mirelle protested, pawing Ellis' orange vest.

"Stay close. We'll be okay," Ellis moved into the cell. A porthole covered in a thin layer of lightsilk looked out on dark water. The void sword's hilt was so cold that ice formed on Ellis' hands when she plunged them into the water, but she had no other choice. She thrust the blade into the water and pushed it into the hull.

As she sliced through the metal, the water pressure pushed the raw edges inward. When she was done, Ellis gasped for breath. The water was at her neck, and the life vest had lifted her onto her toes. Mirelle was half-screaming and half-babbling in the water behind her. Ellis returned the sword to the scabbard. They wouldn't be able to swim through the gap until the pressure equalized.

Mirelle was breathing hard, and Ellis put a hand on her back.

"The life vest is plenty buoyant for both of us. We just have to get out."

Mirelle nodded frantically, eyes wide with fear. Connor spoke to her as the water rose past their necks, but the force was dwindling.

"Let's go," Ellis directed. "We'll duck into the hole and push away. The life jacket will float us up to the surface."

Mirelle nodded again, and they ducked below the water, pushing forward to grip the curled metal edge where the void sword had sliced through the hull. Ellis kept her hand on Mirelle's shirt, and they kicked through the hole, trying not to let the current rake their exposed limbs against the sharp edges.

The life vest's buoyancy overcame the pressure, tugging Ellis upward. She tightened her grip on Mirelle as they rushed up. There were a horrible few seconds of darkness, but finally, they reached the surface. Mirelle frantically thrashed, gasping for breath and pushing Ellis below the surface in her panic. Surrounded by darkness, Ellis' lungs burned. Ice formed on the scabbard on her back, and her vision dimmed.

Ellis dug her nails into Mirelle's arms and clawed toward the surface. "*Stop!*" she screamed after taking a breath. Mirelle stopped thrashing, and Ellis regained control by grabbing Mirelle's collar. "Float on your back. I won't let you go under."

Mirelle's body relaxed fractionally, and she was able to bob on the waves without taking both of them down. Connor swam over and helped, but the sky was dark, and the swells were getting larger. Even though the life jacket held them above the water, they were inundated by waves. Connor and Ellis kicked away from the sinking ship, although it was descending too slowly to create much downward suction.

The shadow magic goggles were still on Ellis' forehead. Pulling them over her eyes, she scanned the sea. As she bobbed to the top of a large wave, she saw a purple glow in the distance, along with the round edge of a hard-shelled inflatable boat. It had to be Sebastian.

"*Hey!*" Ellis screamed before she remembered that her hush puppy was active. She reached into her pocket and found it, struggling to find the off button. "*Hey!*" she shouted again. This time, she thought Sebastian heard her. There was a flash of movement before she fell into the trough between waves.

A minute later, the boat's smooth nose almost hit her in the face.

"Ellis!" Sebastian cried. Mirelle stayed calm long enough to be dragged into the boat, and Ellis and Connor followed. Cold and shivering, they huddled on a narrow bench.

"What the hell did you do to my ship, Ellis?" Sebastian demanded angrily.

"Submarine retrofit," Ellis snapped. The *Violet Eel* lurched below the waves, and the Navy boat rocked. Peering through the shadow goggles, she surveyed the scene, rejoicing at the sight of the many purple cloaker bubbles and invisibility spells clustered around the sinking ship. Her plan had worked. Everyone had made it off and into the lifeboats.

"A captain's supposed to go down with his ship," Sebastian stated, eyes shadowed.

"Don't even think about it. I'll tie you to the wheel if I have to," Ellis ground out through chattering teeth.

Sebastian watched the *Eel* but made no attempt to jump overboard. After a long moment, he asked, "What do we do now?"

"We stay invisible."

"This thing's gas tank is half-full, and the lifeboats are just big rubber rafts."

"If we can't get away, someone has to come get us. We could go for help. Is there anyone on shore you trust who could come pick us up?

"No one who would risk the ire of the US Navy."

Movement just below the surface of the water caught Ellis' eyes. There was an eerie squeak at the limits of her hearing, and an oblong mass broke the surface with a spray. Mirelle screamed.

"Calm down. It's a whale," Sebastian explained.

Ellis scratched her chin as its dorsal fin disappeared below the surface. "Let's go find Percy."

He was in a lifeboat with Landon, Trissa, and Ilva, who looked relieved when Ellis popped into existence on Sebastian's apparently empty boat. Water beaded Percy's skin, and his salt-and-pepper hair was wet and bedraggled, but he looked better than the others. His attention was on the ocean rather than on his companions since it was a goldmine of animal life. No one on the life raft looked pleased to see Mirelle, but they kept their mouths shut.

"Percy, I need your help," Ellis began. "To be more precise. I need your friend's help. Someone we just ran into. Can you get in touch with your whale buddy?"

Percy's eyes narrowed. "Why?"

"We need a tow to shore," Ellis clarified nervously. Percy would never agree to her plan if he thought an animal would be hurt, but she didn't see another option.

He protested, "We're twenty miles offshore!"

"We don't have to go all the way. We just need to get far enough to arrange a pickup where the Navy can't see us."

"I'll see what I can do," Percy drawled. He frowned, then lay face-down on the side of the raft, dangling a hand into the water. His expression went from remote to indecipherable.

"Have you spoken to anyone else?" Trissa asked. "I'm worried about Rami and the others in the medical bay."

"We'll have to trust that they got off the boat," Ellis replied. Invisibility spells and cloaker bubbles floated all around the ship, but that was different from taking a full count. They lapsed into silence, lulled by the waves sloshing against metal and rubber. Thanks to the quiet, Ellis heard the first notes of whale song filter up through the water. "Did you hear that?"

"What?" Ilva asked.

"Yes, but not with my ears," Percy replied.

Ellis listened to the next eerie note, which was low at first and rose into higher registers. Apparently, she was the only one on the boat with sensitive enough ears to hear it. A minute later, a sleek shape broke through the water twenty feet from their two-boat flotilla.

Percy's smile was wide. "I should spend more time on the ocean." Starlight glinted off a huge eye in the water. After a moment, he relayed, "She's not enthusiastic."

Water sprayed from the whale's blowhole in an exasperated sigh.

"Why not?" Ellis asked, giving the whale a friendly smile.

"They're not equipped for tugboat work. If she pushes a raft with her nose, she's as likely to tip it over as propel it, and I don't see a way of affixing a rope to her without injuring her."

Ellis nodded.

There was another burst of whale song. This time, everyone heard the eerie descending notes. "She says she might know a guy."

"What the hell does that mean?" Ellis asked. "Like, a person?"

"Not a human. Or a drow. At least, I don't think so. We'll just have to be patient. She's operating on a whole other wavelength." Percy's good cheer annoyed Ellis, but she took a deep breath and settled in to wait. The life raft had a cache of food and water, which Ilva distributed. Ellis was busy testing her teeth on a granola bar so dense it rivaled the inside of a black hole when a new note rose from the ocean. Unlike the whale's song, this was a high-pitched staccato cry.

"Dolphins!" Sebastian pointed over the raft's bow as two silver shapes leapt out of the water in playful arcs.

"Are they as smart as I've heard?" Ellis asked Percy.

He just laughed. Apparently, he was responding to one of the dolphins. She didn't think he'd heard her, but then he said, "Too smart for their own good. I need a rope."

The life raft's cache produced a twenty-foot length of rope. Percy tied an elaborate series of knots in one end. The other, he affixed to a D-ring on the front of the raft.

He then addressed the dolphins. "You sure about this? You'll tell me if it's uncomfortable?"

Their high-pitched cries sounded almost scornful, and after a moment, Percy's raft lurched forward.

"*Yippee!*" he shouted as the raft surged away.

"*Stop!*" Ellis yelled. She thought they hadn't heard, but after a moment, the raft drifted to a stop. Sebastian steered the hard-shelled Navy boat alongside it. "You have to come with us. We have about ten more life rafts to do."

He frowned, and Ellis saw him glance at the water. His

face froze as his mind traveled elsewhere, and then he smiled.

"Can do!"

Percy had often told Ellis that animal brains were not like human brains. It took him a long time to build rapport with, say, a jellyfish or a king cobra. Talking to dogs and cats was easier since, as domesticated animals, they were somewhat attuned to humans.

Dolphins, Percy told them with saucerlike eyes, were on another level.

"Are they as smart as us?" Ellis asked, tossing a knotted rope to a surly, short-bodied dolphin.

"A better question might be, are we as smart as them?" Percy asked and went back to talking to his new friends.

Apparently, they found towing rubber rafts across the ocean fun. More than once, when Ellis threw the knotted end into the water, a cheerful scuffle broke out over who got to go first. She almost cried when she found Charlie in one of the last boats and leapt onto the raft with such enthusiasm that she nearly tipped it over.

"Careful," Charlie cautioned, but he hugged her anyway. They watched as two young dolphins vied for primacy at the bow, and then Ellis returned to the Navy boat.

"Now, now," Percy chided. "You'll all get a turn."

After they affixed a towline to the last rubber raft and it was skipping across the waves, Ellis joined Sebastian at the wheel.

"Let's go." She glanced nervously at the Navy cruiser. The ship's attention was thoroughly occupied with evacuating the *Violet Eel*, but soon the sailors would start to wonder how a boatload of "merchants" had disappeared. If the right officers talked to people with high enough security clearances, they might wise up. Ellis wanted to be gone before that happened.

"Sebastian?" Ellis called.

He was staring at the ocean where the *Violet Eel* had floated. Only the flagpole was still visible, its fake Swedish merchant's banner a colorless wet mess. As they watched, that disappeared.

"Captain," Ellis yelled to get his attention.

When he turned, there was more than fire in his eyes. Above his freckled cheeks, they smoldered with hatred. "You sank my ship," he snarled.

"I'm sorry. I really am." Ellis remembered how she'd felt when the Outpost was destroyed. "It was the safest choice."

Sebastian turned away, and Ellis wondered if he would hate her forever. Whatever he felt, he grabbed the wheel and steered the boat away from the ghost of the *Eel*.

They caught back up quickly—the dolphins were strong, fast swimmers, but they wasted time fighting each other for turns pulling the boat. The non-pulling dolphins swam and jumped in Sebastian's wake.

When they finally stopped, Sebastian used an emergency radio from one of the lifeboats to contact a *Violet Eel* member who had been on shore leave during the wedding. There was some back-and-forth about how to proceed, and Sebastian suggested contacting an old friend who had retired to start a dive company out of Long Beach.

The wait seemed interminable, but eventually, a modest boat appeared on the horizon, its hull bearing a red-and-white dive flag. The boat's captain introduced himself as

Elliot Burns and proceeded to load them efficiently onto his deck.

The crewmembers with enough juice in their magical tanks to cast shadow spells helped sink the life rafts and the hard-shelled attack boat Sebastian had commandeered from the Navy. It felt wasteful, but Sebastian didn't want the Navy finding the boats and asking questions about why Captain Burns had been in the area.

By the time they were done, exhaustion had made Ellis pretty well insensate. As they headed toward the shore, only Sebastian looked back in the direction of the *Violet Eel*.

CHAPTER FOUR

Supplying a ship was a challenging logistics problem. Supplying a crew without a ship was worse. Some of the human and human-passing crew members sensed the desperate circumstances and asked Sebastian for shore leave, but that wasn't an option for the drow or for Percy, who was still a wanted man. After Captain Burns dropped them off in Long Beach, they spent a chaotic night in a cheap motel. It was hard to get enough rooms, and Sebastian maxed out several company credit cards. Even so, the crew was packed in like sardines, and hardly anyone slept. Disagreements became arguments, and one argument turned into a fistfight.

The next morning, Ellis, Charlie, and Percy were eating gas station muffins at a shabby picnic table in the courtyard when Rose approached them. Percy immediately stopped flinging muffin bits at a rangy seagull and gave her his full attention.

"We need a place to stay," she began.

Ellis and Charlie exchanged looks. Rose was a glamorous woman used to luxurious surroundings. However, Ellis didn't think she could stand to hear another complaint. Particularly not when more than half the crew were furious at her for sinking their ship.

"We're doing our best," Ellis soothed. "We'll find something, I promise."

"I'm not here to complain. I'm here because I might have a solution."

"Oh!" Ellis exclaimed.

"One of my former clients has a mansion in Calabasas. His name is Virgil Curaco. If I asked nicely, I think he'd let us borrow the house."

"Virgil Curaco..." The name was familiar. "*The* Virgil Curaco?" The Curaco Group was a multimedia conglomerate. All Ellis knew about it was that its founder was disgustingly wealthy.

Rose sighed. "Yes. That's the one."

Percy's face pinched into a scowl. Rose managed to ignore it until he said, "No siree. That is not a good idea. We don't need some rich asshole all up in our business."

Rose shook her head. "He won't be there. He's summering in Europe, or maybe Macau. I don't know. The man's as rich as Croesus, and he has more houses than friends."

"And he'd just let you borrow the mansion? Indefinitely?" Charlie asked.

"Keep your judgment to yourself," Rose snapped. Charlie closed his mouth and put his hands up in surrender.

"Charlie's right. I don't like it," Percy interjected.

Rose's face was flushed as she turned on him. "This is not about what you like. This is about what we *need*."

"He'll have expectations," Percy mumbled. Picking up on Percy's souring mood, the rangy seagull squawked and flapped onto the table, then plucked the remainder of Percy's muffin out of its wrapper. Rose shrieked and backed away, glaring at Percy. Under her gaze, he wilted.

"If you have a ten-bedroom Calabasas mansion you'd like to loan me, you can have expectations, too," Rose said.

Percy returned her glare for a moment, then scrambled to his feet. Muttering something about a muffin, he fled toward the gas station on the corner.

"Should I make the call?" Rose asked. She sounded wounded.

"Yeah," Ellis replied. "Do you need a phone?"

"No. Mine's in a waterproof case. Men are constantly throwing me into pools." She huffed and stalked away, phone in her hand.

"She's lucky," Charlie murmured.

Ellis put her hand on his. "If you're that desperate, *I'll* throw you into a pool."

"I mean, she's lucky her phone still works," Charlie clarified. Almost all of them had lost their phones in the ocean. Sebastian had made a run to Walmart to buy a mix of replacements and burners, but Ellis still felt disconnected.

Rose's call bore fruit, and by that afternoon, the *Violet Eel's* crewmembers were stuffed into a wide range of vehicles headed north up the Pacific Coast Highway.

Ellis wasn't thrilled about the loaner mansion for different reasons than Percy. Rose confirmed that the owner was away—in Monaco, not Macau—but the mansion had a small army of staff, all of whom had to be paid go-away money. Mostly, they were happy for the paid vacation, except for an exacting majordomo whose sense of self was clearly linked to his job. Even he had a price point, however, and eventually, they moved in.

Over the next several days, Ellis wondered if this was what a vacation was like. She had no responsibilities. Sebastian's security team had taken over guarding Mirelle, and Emily had roundly rejected her offers to help with the cooking. Sebastian was attempting to cure the rest of his crew's boredom via the time-honored naval tradition of plying them with huge volumes of hard alcohol. Tension simmered beneath the party atmosphere, though, and Ellis wondered when it would all boil over.

"It's hard to save up for a new ship when I'm paying a pool boy *not* to clean the pool," Sebastian grumbled, feet splashing in the pool. It was hard to take his complaints seriously when they were uttered between large gulps of mojito.

"The chores will keep us busy. And it's better than having the place overrun with strangers," Rose mused.

On a one-man mission to fish half-drowned bees out of the pool, Percy was industriously ignoring her. Rose's plunging emerald-green one-piece made that difficult, but he stuck to his guns.

Half the crew was treating the mansion like a vacation rental, and half were treating it like their new ship. In mourning for the *Eel* and lacking his first officer, Sebastian wasn't providing much leadership. Emily was running the galley with rigid military efficiency, but she refused to serve them poolside, stating that "This isn't fucking Club Med."

The mansion was large, but the crew was larger. Even with ten bedrooms, they didn't have much privacy. Ellis and Charlie had barely had a moment alone since their arrival, although they'd shared meals and spent a lot of time together. None of it, however, had been intimate. Now, he emerged from the main house with two large, umbrella-adorned plastic glasses. "Mojito?"

Ellis grinned and accepted the drink. As she sipped it, she sized up the intimidating rectangle of turquoise water before her. She had survived several recent dunks in the Pacific, so why did it make her nervous? Sebastian was angry and withdrawn, and she hoped that a task might focus him.

"I want to learn to swim," Ellis announced. "Landon and Trissa should learn, too. And anyone else who wants to."

Sebastian looked up blearily. Bottomless mojitos were not the best warmup for swim lessons. "Tomorrow," Ellis added. "First thing in the morning. Swim class. I'll tell the others."

Trissa was enthusiastic. Landon, who hated formal education, grumbled but reluctantly agreed it was a good idea. Connor and Ilva promised to show up, too.

The swim lesson the next morning was a family affair. Even hungover, Sebastian was an excellent teacher. His instructions washed over her as she floated on her back with her eyes closed against the punishing sun. It was actually pleasant. Much better than being thrashed by waves in a dark ocean.

It was hard for Ellis to relax, however. She had placed

the void sword and scabbard at the side of the pool, and as she floated, it wanted her attention. She wouldn't be comfortable until it was strapped on her body again.

"All right," Sebastian continued. "Let's get our faces wet."

They had just flipped over and were blowing bubbles through their noses and mouths while holding onto the side of the pool when the purr of a car engine filtered through the water. Ellis looked at Sebastian, lost her composure as she remembered she couldn't actually swim yet, and thrashed in panic until she remembered the pool wasn't very deep. With her chin above the surface, she looked in the direction of the noise.

"That's Virgil's Bugatti," Rose announced from a nearby pool chair, a deep frown line appearing between her eyebrows.

"I thought he was in Monaco?" Ellis asked.

"So did I." Rose retrieved a silky cover-up, then paused. Wondering, perhaps, if she might get a warmer reception without it. After a moment of indecision, she threw the robe on and headed toward the garage.

Sebastian was barking orders at nearby crewmembers from halfway up the pool steps. The Speedo failed to diminish his command presence. "Disappear!" he shouted at Connor and Ilva. No one had been expecting visitors.

Scrambling onto the wet concrete after Sebastian, Ellis made sure her family was out of sight behind an invisibility spell. Then, she took a long sip of shadow magic potion from a bottle on a nearby table, pulled a spell around herself, and headed for the garage. *Invisibility is the ultimate pool cover-up.*

She arrived to see a bald, spray-tanned man pull Rose into a more-than-friendly embrace. That must be her former client.

"Rose, my blossom, my flower!" One hand crept beneath her silky wrap.

Rose put her cheek in the path of his diving lips and slipped out of his embrace with a lithe efficiency that Ellis envied. She would have punched the guy. Rose de-escalated. Ellis decided that if Rose ever wanted a new career, she would be a terrific vigilante.

"I thought you were in Monaco?" Rose asked, tone friendly but not inviting. "Is this a new paint job?" she asked, circling the aforementioned Bugatti in a way that put distance between them. Looking at herself in the car's high-gloss red paint, she tucked a lock of hair behind her ear.

The bald man looked nonplussed. "Nah, I keep a spare at the airfield. The black Bugatti's in the auxiliary garage."

What the hell is an auxiliary garage?

"To what do I owe the pleasure? Did something come up?" Rose asked cautiously.

"I couldn't stay away from my Rosie. It's been too long." Virgil circled toward her. His eyes were hungry.

A gray flash caught Ellis' eye as a squirrel darted into the garage behind Virgil. Ellis recognized the intelligent look in its eyes. Uh-oh. Percy was watching.

Rose noticed the squirrel, too, but her attention quickly moved to an incoming cloud of songbirds. Ellis thought the flock would attack Virgil, and if that happened, she would give Percy a stern talking-to. However, the birds circled above the Bugatti. Within seconds, a monsoon of white poop strafed the shining paint.

"*What the hell!*" Virgil screamed. More birds were flying into the garage, blocking Ellis' view of Virgil's shiny and rapidly reddening scalp. The media mogul grabbed a broom and swiped it at them, but the birds dodged.

Ellis stared in awe at the, erm, *whitewashed* car. *What the hell were those birds eating?*

Virgil was so busy trying to shoo away the birds that he failed to notice the army of squirrels encroaching on his ankles. Their nails dug into his bespoke summer-weight wool pants as they climbed toward the lush chest hair peeking out of his deep-V-neck silk shirt. When they reached skin, they bit him.

"*What the fuck!*" Virgil shouted, spinning and swatting at the squirrels.

Rose was irritated, but she made no move to help the billionaire. Neither did Ellis. Virgil's presence at the mansion was a problem, and as far as she knew, no one had ever died by squirrel attack.

"That's enough," Rose stated in a low voice, arms crossed. Whether she was speaking to Percy or the squirrels, they got the message. Fanning out from Virgil's body like they were escaping a fire, they chittered and fled. The birds went with them, leaving Virgil panting in tattered clothes, his skin covered in squirrel bites.

"You'd better get those bites looked at," Rose told the man cheerfully and held out her hand. "Come on. I'll take you to the hospital."

"I don't like other people driving my Bugatti," Virgil countered pathetically.

"We can wait for an ambulance if you want, but it'll take them ages to get here. Some of those squirrels looked rabid, and you'll want to get your shots right away. Plus, I've heard there's bubonic plague going around California's rodent populations."

Virgil slumped but didn't release his keys.

"If you let me take you to the hospital, I'll kiss those nasty squirrel bites and make them all better," Rose offered, the edge in her voice clearly meant for Percy. Virgil was cheered by this offer. Reluctantly, he handed over the keys.

"Let's go," Rose climbed in.

CHAPTER FIVE

Ellis found Percy tucked between two hedges in the garden, hand-feeding his impromptu squirrel army leftover ham sandwiches from lunch. Several of the furry rodent warriors were lapping some pale green liquid out of a shallow bowl.

"Are you feeding those squirrels mojitos?" Ellis demanded.

"They worked hard today," Percy shot back defensively.

"Using alcohol to soothe the horrors of war." Ellis shook her head sadly. "Are you okay? It's not like you to use animals like that. Not unless there's an emergency."

"It *was* an emergency. We couldn't let him see the drow quartered in his mansion," Percy explained stiffly.

"Uh-huh." Ellis sighed. "Well, try not to let your menagerie get mixed up in any more private revenge."

He looked ashamed. "How did Rose seem when she left?" Percy asked after a long silence. "Was she sorry he was hurt?" A nearby squirrel squeaked enthusiastically.

"Rose doesn't like to see *anyone* hurt," Ellis scolded and left Percy to his squirrel bacchanal.

Virgil's sudden appearance made clear what they should have known all along: they didn't have time for a weeks-long pool party in Calabasas. Picking up on the shifting mood, Emily stopped making mojitos and started brewing pots of coffee. Sebastian and the family tried to resume their swimming lesson, but everyone was too distracted to make much progress.

Later that evening, Rose returned to the mansion, reporting that Virgil would be in the hospital for several days getting preventative treatment for a host of rodent-borne illnesses. Unfortunately, he'd also made noise about contacting exterminators to take care of the squirrel problem. This news set Percy on a mission to disperse the local wildlife.

"Serves him right," Rose grumbled, then added, "Although I hope none of those squirrels got hurt."

Sebastian and his crew had not made any headway in finding Val. She didn't have friends or family outside the *Eel*. Ellis found that unbelievable and questioned half a dozen crew members about it. They all confirmed their captain's assertion.

When Sebastian forced Val to take shore leave, which wasn't often because of the raging fuss she made about it, she went to an Airbnb near Yosemite, dividing her time between hiking in the park and perfecting her marksmanship at a local shooting range. Sebastian called the owners of both the Airbnb and the shooting range, but no one had seen her.

Sebastian maintained that the Navy cruiser had been an

accident. "If Val had wanted to destroy us, she would have. I think she made a simple escape attempt, and we got unlucky." He was sitting on a barstool in the kitchen, drinking Emily's excellent coffee.

"Does it really matter where she is?" Ellis asked. "If she wanted to disappear, that's not a problem."

Sebastian's eye twitched, and his fist clenched around the coffee cup. Ellis knew she'd offended him. Sebastian's bond with Val was deep, and he couldn't accept that she'd gone to ground without saying goodbye.

"I mean, it's not an apocalyptic problem. If she stays off the grid, no one's going to die. And she could do it, right?"

"She has years of Special Ops experience and a handful of contacts that even *I* don't know about," Sebastian admitted. "It's possible but not likely, especially considering the data theft."

"We'll try to find her," Ellis mused. "But we have to focus on the worst-case scenario."

"The one where she releases the information she stole from the Violet Eye?" Sebastian asked.

"Exactly. You spent a long time strategizing, right? I doubt she'll reinvent the wheel, so what resources would she need to execute your plans? What contacts might she go to?"

"There's a reporter at the LA Times," Sebastian offered after a long moment. "Name's Kip Acosta. A local. He's met some of the drow from the *Violet Eel*. Used to cover war zones, which Val related to. They had a rapport. He agreed to sit on the story until we were ready to release."

"It sounds like he's our guy." Ellis grinned tightly. "We should go check him out."

Sebastian nodded.

"I'll go with you," Connor suggested.

"So will I!"

Ellis turned in surprise and found Percy loitering in the doorway. His shoulders were slumped, and he was fiddling with the bottom of his shirt.

"If we find Val, you can't sic a bunch of rabid squirrels on her," Ellis warned.

"Cross my heart and hope to die. Besides, Rose and I need a little time to cool off."

"You think she'll loan us the Bugatti?" Ellis asked with a grin.

Sebastian shook his head. "It'll attract too much attention. Also, I'd rather not waste time at the carwash."

Ellis sighed. He was right. Stealth was more important than speed.

"Speaking of not attracting attention, what's the cloaker situation?"

"They're maintained and ready to go," Sebastian told her. "Don't lose them, though."

"I wouldn't dream of it. Percy, why don't you come with me? I've got a present for you."

CHAPTER SIX

Percy was delighted by his new cloaker. He flicked it on and off with such rapidity that Connor threatened to take it away from him. He settled down after they parked, however. The mood in the vicinity of the stolid LA Times office building was subdued as the four invisibly approached their destination. Journalists worked late, but usually not *this* late. Only two windows were lit on the upper floors, yellow squares like watching eyes. Planes took off and landed across the highway at LAX, making the air thick and smoggy.

Ellis' skin prickled. Someone was watching her. She searched the building's windows for signs of surveillance but found none. She couldn't figure out why she was spooked, but she hadn't survived as a vigilante by ignoring her gut. "I want to do a perimeter sweep. Someone's watching us."

Sebastian surveyed the empty streets doubtfully. "There's no one here."

"I trust my daughter's instincts," Connor interjected. "We should do the sweep."

Sebastian threw up his hands, and they made a slow loop of the building. It wasn't true that no one was around. A homeless man camping catty-corner to the building's entrance cursed as he paced back and forth in front of his tent.

"Give me a minute." Ellis held up a hand for the others to stop. She pulled a shadow magic cloak around herself and adjusted the position of the scabbard on her back. Her father had questioned her wisdom in bringing the ancient magical weapon on a reconnaissance mission, but Ellis argued that it was safer with her than anywhere else. Truthfully, she wasn't sure she could have left it at the mansion if she had tried.

Sebastian had brought one of the dart guns that had made it off the *Violet Eel*. A more sensible weapon for a heavily populated civilian area, Ellis decided. The sword shivered disdainfully.

Approaching the tent, she looked the man over. Something was different from the unhoused people she'd encountered in the past. Crouching, she watched him for a minute. His tent was torn, but not at the seams. It looked like the material had been stabbed and ripped by hand. The edges of the tent where it touched the ground were clean, although the material higher up had been dirtied, apparently at random.

The man was watching the Times building; that much was clear. When a woman with a chihuahua passed him on the way to the apartment complexes further south, he barely looked at her. In contrast, when the door of the Times building opened, his head whipped toward the movement. Ellis continued watching for another minute before she realized what had raised her internal alarms. She returned to the others.

"That guy is military." She pointed at the tent.

"How do you know?" Sebastian asked.

"How many homeless guys do you know with brand new French manicures?" Ellis asked.

Connor frowned. "How many Special Ops agents do you know with brand new French manicures?"

Sebastian shrugged. "Snipers take care of their hands."

"Well, he's not a sniper," Ellis said. "Or not a very effective one. Percy, can you keep an eye on him?"

Percy nodded. Seconds later, an odd-eyed and extremely ugly pigeon fluttered down from a lamp post and hopped across the sidewalk in front of them, pecking at invisible crumbs.

"*Wormy!*" Ellis whispered.

"She wanted to come," Percy explained. The pigeon looked in their direction, cocking her head. "Does the cloaker work on animals, too?"

"It works on their vision, not their sense of smell. For the most part," Ellis clarified. Percy nodded.

Sebastian sighed. "If my lab wasn't at the bottom of the Pacific Ocean, we could work on scent blockers."

"It's called deodorant, and someone already invented it. Let's go," Ellis ordered.

"Wait!" Percy hissed. He had a faraway look in his eyes, tuned in to a wavelength none of the rest had access to.

"One of the local birds says there's a guy on that rooftop." He pointed. "I think he's got a gun."

It was dark, and if the barrel of a sniper rifle was poking out over the top of the building, they were too blinded by the streetlights to see it. "I could go up there and take him out," Ellis offered.

"That would let them know for sure that we're here," Sebastian countered. "We're better off staying under the radar. I'm going to risk going in."

"Are you sure that's a good idea?" Connor asked.

"No, but Kip deserves a heads-up. I'll sneak him out of the building if I can."

"Then I'm going with you," Ellis stated. "Percy, stay on surveillance. Dad, get ready to intervene if French Manicure makes a move."

Connor nodded, and Ellis and Sebastian headed toward the building. The front door was going to be a problem. The soldiers watching the building would notice if it opened and closed without anyone going through.

"We'll just have to wait," Ellis told her companion.

Finally, a light went on, and there was movement behind the glass. Sebastian yanked Ellis to her feet, and as the door opened, they sprinted toward it across the bedraggled lawn. As Ellis' feet hit concrete again, an invisible weight slammed into her shins, sending her flying into a blue USPS mailbox. There was a loud clang, and chips of blue paint rained onto the concrete around her body.

Shit.

She hadn't turned on her hush puppy, and the fall had made a lot of noise. Halfway through a string of muttered obscenities, an arm wrapped around her neck and cut off her air supply. Ellis thrashed in the stranglehold.

"Calm the fuck down," a familiar voice ordered.

"Vlgghhh?" Ellis asked, which was the closest she could get to "Val" with an ulna across her windpipe.

"Val!" Sebastian exclaimed, popping into the envelope of Ellis' cloaker.

The arm around her neck loosened enough for her to peer at French Manicure. He was watching them intently. "They can hear us." Ellis directed Val's attention across the street. "We've got to get out of here."

Val hesitated, clearly tempted to crush Ellis' windpipe and be done with it, but she relented. As they scurried around the corner, a bullet took a chunk out of the sidewalk they'd just abandoned.

When they were behind cover, Ellis caught her breath and assessed the situation. Sebastian's first officer—or possibly, *former* first officer—was wearing shadow goggles, and her compact frame was dwarfed by a green military surplus jacket. Now Ellis knew how Val had been able to see them. Val stuffed her hands into her pockets and leaned against the building.

Sebastian looked like he couldn't decide if he wanted to kiss Val or murder her. He flicked on his hush puppy and shook her. "What the fuck, Val?"

"Captain," she replied drily.

"Where's the data from the Violet Eye?" Sebastian demanded. "Don't bullshit me. I'm sure you've noticed that we've got company," He swept an arm at the tent encampment and the building across the street.

"I didn't know about the sniper," she protested.

"No shit," Sebastian shot back.

"Someone must have intercepted our communications with Kip. Makes speed even more important."

"Speed? For what?"

Val's eyes drifted north, where a jetliner was descending toward LAX. She pressed her lips together.

"What did you do?" Sebastian demanded.

There was a moment of silence. "You should get back to the ship."

"*There is no ship!*" Sebastian yelled with such ferocity that Ellis layered a muffling spell on top of his hush puppy. "You left us in the water like a sitting duck. Then a Navy cruiser boarded us, and Ellis went full iceberg on the hull. We had to use dolphins to escape!"

After a pause, Val burst out laughing. Sebastian fumed as she slapped her knee. "*Dolphins?* Oh, man, you really had me going."

"It's not a joke!" Sebastian exclaimed. His freckles were red enough to light a cigarette.

Val realized he wasn't being funny. "Shit. What? What do you mean, 'dolphins?'"

"Majestic, big brains, blowholes?" Sebastian growled. "We used them to tow the lifeboats."

"We need the *Eel*," Val whispered, pupils dilated with fear.

"I know!"

"How are we going to protect everyone?" Val asked.

"Protect everyone from *what?*" Sebastian demanded.

The orange sodium streetlights illuminated the manic brightness in her eyes. Val was breathing hard and shrinking away from them.

Her hand came out of her pocket, and Ellis saw metal and plastic. She raised a hand to protect herself, but it was too late. There was a whirr of compressed air, and a sharp point pricked her stomach. Ellis tried to make sense of what was happening, but her eyes lost the ability to focus, and her drooping head pulled her down into the concrete, then into a deeper blackness.

CHAPTER SEVEN

She woke up to feral chittering, so she expected to be outside when she opened her eyes. She was in the Camry they had rented, slumped in the backseat. A furry black-masked raccoon was staring at her from between the front seats.

"Hello," Ellis greeted in confusion. She panicked and reached behind her, feeling for the sword at her back. When the cold scabbard met her fingers, she relaxed.

Percy's face appeared above the raccoon's. "Some asshole darted you. Seeing as how we let you take the only pair of shadow goggles with you, you were a bitch to find. Fortunately, Zorro here has an exceptional sense of smell and was able to nose you out."

Connor, who was in the driver's seat, looked grim. "I told him not to allow the rodent in the car, but Percy said it was rude to leave a man behind."

"Good man," Sebastian whispered. He looked like he'd been awake for longer than Ellis.

Connor cleared his throat.

"What?" Ellis rasped.

"There was more sniper fire."

"Is anyone hurt?"

"Only the city's sidewalk repair budget." Percy affectionately scratched Zorro's head. The raccoon looked like it regretted getting in the car.

"What happened, exactly?"

"Val darted us and escaped." Sebastian groaned as he sat upright.

"What the fuck are we going to do now?" Ellis asked.

Zorro squeaked insistently.

"Zorro wants a ride to the cemetery." Percy sighed. "He's friends with some feral cats there. After that, I suggest we get something to eat."

They swung past the entrance of the Inglewood cemetery. It was closed, but the raccoon didn't seem to mind. When they opened the door, he skittered outside and scaled a tall rectangular hedge without looking back. A few blocks away, they parked outside a half-empty Guatemalan restaurant, in which TVs blared from every corner.

"What do you want us to get you, Dad?" Ellis asked. It was too risky for Connor to come inside with them.

"I want to eat a proper meal in a proper chair," Connor stated. Ellis was about to protest when he fished a gold medallion etched with fungal whorls out of his pocket. When Ellis peeked at it using the shadow goggles, it nearly blinded her.

"I've been saving this for a special occasion." Connor slipped it over his neck, and a second later, her father was an unremarkable brown-haired human male. Ellis wondered if they should save the medallion for a nonrestaurant-related situation, but her father looked exhausted. Sometimes, dinner was an emergency.

The food came out quickly, and they tucked into stacks of pupusas, including a vegan black bean option for Percy. Ellis topped one of the thick pork-stuffed cakes with cabbage and doused it in the cool tomato salsa that accompanied the order, washing everything down with cold soda. She had wanted to get a pitcher of beer, but Sebastian said they shouldn't so soon after being drugged. Ellis had protested but settled for sugar and caffeine.

The first sign that something was really wrong was that all the televisions in the restaurant went blue at the same time. They'd been playing different channels, so Ellis assumed there had been a problem with the Wi-Fi or cable.

The second sign that something was wrong was the fight in the kitchen. At first, it was just shouting, but then pots clanged, and two men burst out. They both looked afraid, but one looked more afraid than the other. He threw off his apron and sprinted for the front door, screaming in Spanish. His coworker shouted after him but quickly gave up the chase in favor of staring at his phone. The woman who had taken their order joined him, and the two huddled over the screen.

"*Excuse me,*" Ellis shouted. The server, who had previously been friendly, flashed her a dirty look and ignored her. Ellis discovered what the fuss was about when the televisions turned back on. News anchors, some of whom looked like they'd been pushed onscreen before hair and makeup were done, stared fearfully at their teleprompters. **BREAKING NEWS** flashed on the chyron.

Ellis focused on the nearest anchor, a blonde woman in

a red dress whose face was pale beneath her bronzer. "The information we're about to share is not a joke. It might sound outrageous, but it is real. We will be here to help you understand it. We have just received credible information that a second humanoid species has been discovered on Earth."

A video played. Ellis gaped.

It was Rami. He was smiling and waving at the camera with a blue hand.

"Shit," Sebastian muttered under his breath. In the video, Rami had both arms, which meant the video had been filmed some time ago.

"Discovered?" Ellis asked so loudly that the two people hunched over the cell phone behind the counter glanced at her. She dropped her voice to a whisper. "What the hell do they mean, *discovered*? We've been here the whole time."

"Did you do this?" Connor asked Sebastian, who shook his head.

"From the looks of it, Val spammed out our press kit," Sebastian explained.

The newscaster's voice was reedy as she continued, "Some claim these individuals are a previously unknown species indigenous to Earth. Others wonder if they are aliens. In both cases, these individuals, who call themselves the drow, have advanced technological capabilities, including the ability to turn invisible."

Ellis wouldn't describe shadow magic as technological, but the reporters were in a tight spot. "We've just learned about magic elves living under Los Angeles" was a much harder sell.

A familiar voice blared from the TV speakers. "Hello. My name is Rami, and I'm a drow."

"Where's the rest of the vid kit?" Sebastian growled, eyes fixed on the nearest screen.

"Which part?" Ellis asked.

"The adorable smiling drow kids." Sebastian gripped the edge of the table.

"Smiling kids don't sell cable TV subscriptions. Fear does." Percy twisted a sugar packet anxiously between his fingers until it broke open. "They didn't release a photo of drow looking sinister or dangerous, though."

The video of Rami dissolved. A map of the United States with several large red dots replaced it. "According to the information received by our news desk," the anchor continued, "drow communities are located in several spots across the United States."

The big red dot in the middle of the Angeles National Forest made Ellis sick. "They're making this sound like a dirty secret. Not something the drow chose to share."

"Val really fucked us over. We weren't supposed to rush." Sebastian yanked his phone out of his pocket and typed anxiously. "The website's down."

"What website?" Ellis asked.

"The one we built for the launch. It was supposed to go live when we made the announcement. It had all kinds of information. Interviews. Music. Rami's tunnel bar recipe. We created it so that if the news twisted things, people could look for themselves. Why the fuck isn't the website up?"

"The military asked the ISP to shut it down?" Percy suggested. "Or maybe it got overloaded with traffic."

Connor, who had not spoken the whole time, looked away from the screen. The medallion muted his expression. Ellis was about to ask him what he thought when he reached up and pulled the medallion off his neck. His pale tan flesh turned a mottled purple, and his hair bleached back to silver-white. "I did not ask for this day, but I will not shy away from it." Connor climbed out of the booth. Drawing himself to his full height, he spread his arms. "Excuse me!"

The server and the cook didn't look up from the phone, which was blaring a Spanish-language news program.

"Oh, my God!" someone shouted. A woman at a table on the other end of the restaurant had seen Connor. She froze in shock, then raised her phone and began filming.

"Excuse me!" Connor repeated. This time, he caught the server's attention.

She screamed and sprinted into the kitchen.

"My name is Connor Burton. I am a member of the Swallow's Nest drow community. We seek friendship, not conflict."

A slightly better showing than "We come in peace" or "Take us to your leader." The man behind the counter looked unconvinced. He dove for something and reemerged with a shotgun.

Ellis' stomach twisted, but Connor was quick on the uptake and popped out of existence as birdshot peppered the room.

"You're going to kill someone!" Ellis shouted at the man with the shotgun. He was too afraid to listen.

"*Get out of here!*" he shouted, pointing the shotgun at the doors and backing toward the kitchen.

Ellis and the others scrambled outside, although she held the door open for a few extra seconds. Then she dove into the driver's seat. When they were in the car, Connor popped back into existence.

"That went poorly," he remarked, face neutral.

"Let's save the close encounters of the third kind until things settle down," Ellis suggested.

"Very well." After a moment, Connor broke the tension by holding out a plate he'd swiped from the restaurant. "Did everyone get enough pupusas?"

Ellis didn't want to start a possible apocalypse by turning down food, so she helped finish the pupusas before putting the car in gear and heading back toward Calabasas. It took a long time to reach PCH.

Wreckage from accidents dotted the streets, and police were not responding. The only people they saw outside were rushing to and from cars. In a strip mall, a couple was boarding over the windows of an antique shop. Ellis was tempted to yell out the window that the drow didn't want to steal their shitty mid-century modern knockoffs.

Most of the lights inside the houses they passed were off, although televisions were occasionally visible through curtains or blinds, all on news channels.

Sebastian dove into his phone and stayed there, scrolling through TikTok reactions to the news. On one, a woman sang an acoustic guitar cover of John Lennon's *Imagine*, only instead of "people," she said, "purple." Conspiracy-theory YouTubers rejected the news release right and left, insisting that the government had created a hoax as a pretext to impose martial law.

"Imagine all the purple, living life in peace. You ooh ooohhhhh."

Ellis' mind raced as she waited at a red light. "They have the location of the Homestead. How long until they find the entrance?"

Her new phone, a burner from one of Sebastian's replenishment runs, rang. Ellis hadn't had time to program any numbers into it, so she picked it up on faith.

"Ellis?" Charlie asked. He sounded like he was on edge.

"What is it?"

"I called Liza and Oscar. The LAPD was told to evacuate a wide area around the Angeles National Forest. They said the brass is being tight-lipped, but there's a military attaché in the building."

"Any chance the military is gearing up to support a diplomatic envoy?" Ellis asked drily, then sighed. "Ugh. We've got to get in touch with Chan." She braked hard as she swerved onto the shoulder.

Percy, who had only heard Ellis' half of the conversation, ripped the phone out of her hands. "No, ma'am. Oh, no, you don't. That woman is a, pardon my language, *politician*, and she cannot be trusted more than most politicians cannot be trusted, which is saying something."

"Yeah, but she knows us, and she knows the drow," Ellis argued. "Whatever her flaws, she knows we're not monsters or animals."

Percy glared. "She was going to lock us up forever."

Ellis watched a Tesla hit a light post. When the screech of rubber on asphalt quieted, she continued, "Well, we *did* punch a few holes in her bioweapons facility."

"I don't like any of this," Charlie insisted. "The DRI was

a small operation. The institution might have disbanded, but its knowledge didn't disappear. Plenty of soldiers and scientists remember how to fight drow, and soon the whole military will know."

"They left their lightsilk in the building, and we destroyed most of it."

"I'll bet you a million bucks they're busy making more," Charlie shot back. "Or they will be in about two hours."

Ellis didn't take that bet. "That's why we need to find her *now*. Can you help, Percy? Hack into her emails and find out where she is?"

"I don't need to," Percy countered.

"Why not?"

He held up his phone. The chyron scrolling across the bottom read, **CHAN TO GIVE ADDRESS AT CITY HALL.**

"What time?" Ellis asked.

"Eight A.M."

They had a lot of time to kill before then. "It could be a trap," Connor pointed out.

"Well, then we'll have to be careful not to spring it." Ellis put the car in gear and yanked the wheel into a screeching U-turn.

"*Stop!*" Percy shouted.

Ellis stopped in the middle of the road, ignoring the Humvee behind her laying on its horn. "What is it?"

"Your people live out in the forest, right?" Percy asked.

"The drow?"

"Technically, they live *under* the forest, but yes. All the entrances are out there."

"Well, forests are full of animals, so nobody's better

positioned to keep an eye on things than yours truly. I can build a wild network, but I gotta be close."

"We have to get to Chan before her speech. There's no time."

"I know. Let me out here, and I'll find my own way."

"By 'Find your own way,' do you mean you're going to steal a car?"

"No!" Percy protested, then coughed. "Technically, I'm going to *hijack* a car."

"What!"

Percy shrugged. "I don't have the time or equipment for digital hotwiring, and the police are distracted right now." He was right. Hijacking wouldn't be on the top of the LAPD's priority list any time soon.

She was reluctant to let Percy go off on his own, but they needed someone to keep an eye on the territory around the Homestead. "Just…be careful," Ellis warned. Percy grinned and clambered out of the car.

To Ellis' surprise, Connor went with him. "I'm going, too."

"No! You can't!"

"This is the greatest threat the Homestead has faced in my lifetime. I will not abandon my people. Percy doesn't know the terrain, and I'm not sure he's much of a camper."

Ellis didn't want her dad to leave, but he was right. They all had to protect the drow in their own way. "Good luck. Call if you need anything."

Connor nodded. Percy was already halfway down the street, angling toward a harried-looking man rushing out of a nearby apartment building with car keys in his hand.

"*Hello, sir!*" Percy shouted, waving to get the man's attention. Connor went invisible.

Godspeed, Ellis thought. As she drove away, she tried to ignore the man's angry screams. The evening's chaos had settled into an uncomfortable stasis. The streets had, by and large, emptied. Still, she remained alert as she drove downtown, doubling back a few times to get around blocked streets. When they were two blocks away from City Hall, they settled in to wait, taking turns sleeping.

Around three A.M., Ellis jolted awake to the ringing of a phone. It turned out to be Sebastian's, not hers, and he took the call with bleary-eyed reluctance. Ellis watched his face fall as he talked.

"What is it?" she asked when he hung up.

"That was Emily back at the mansion. Mirelle escaped."

"What? *How?*"

"The guards thought that as long as she used magic, she'd be secure. Apparently, she picked the lock on the lightsilk cuffs the old-fashioned way."

Ellis wanted to go bust some heads. Lock-picking was an old drow tradition in the Swallow's Nest. "Stupid," she grumbled.

"I agree, but there's not much we can do about it now."

They would worry about a manhunt later. The news made it even harder for Ellis to sleep, but she managed a bad hour or two. At dawn, she and Sebastian climbed out of the car and made their way the final blocks to City Hall.

The gathering crowd was patchy. Terrified Angelenos wanted to stay in, not watch a politician jaw about how they all needed to work together for the common good. A large percentage of the throng had wandered over from Skid Row, so the small audience was rough.

As the sun hit the courtyard, Ellis sipped shadow magic potion.

"Hey, sweetheart. Wanna share?" A man with rotten teeth snaked an arm around Ellis' waist and grabbed for the bottle, assuming it contained liquor.

"You have three seconds to let go, or I break your fingers into bone shards," Ellis snarled. Taking one look at her expression, the man released the bottle and stumbled away.

"Good choice. This stuff's an acquired taste anyway." She put distance between them and blended into the crowd. "We have to get inside the building," Ellis whispered to Sebastian. He nodded and pushed into the crowd. Moving slowly, they cased the building.

Chan had plenty of security support, but none of it appeared to be DRI-flavored.

Ellis scrutinized the buzz-cut brigade on the front steps for flashes of lightsilk or funnel-shaped confetti guns. All she saw was body armor and bullets. Turning invisible, she and Sebastian leapt over the security rope that circled the building. From there, they traversed the lawn to the back of the building, stopping when they reached an arched window well-concealed by a decorative shrub.

There, Ellis used shadow magic to cut a careful hole in the glass and slithered through, pulling Sebastian behind her. They entered a vaulted rotunda with an elaborate floor mosaic featuring a central image of a sailing ship. Although all the lights were on, the building seemed abandoned.

"What do we do?" Sebastian asked. His voice echoed in the room, and Ellis gestured for him to flick on his hush puppy, then listened until she heard the faint sound of voices.

"This way." Ellis followed the noise. As they approached the western side of the building, the voices got louder. Rounding a corner, she spotted a large group of people in a small office. *Bingo.*

The door was open, although a severe-looking muscular man was stationed in front of it. Ellis looked past him and assessed Chan's companions. Political types, from the looks of things, although you never knew which aides did Krav Maga.

Cloakers and invisibility spells provided excellent cover in open terrain and were good for general concealment, but they were tricky in tight spaces. When Sebastian went through the door, much of the guard's body would be inside the cloaker's envelope. If he turned his head or bent down to tie his shoe at the wrong time, he might see Sebastian.

"You have your dart gun?" Ellis asked.

Sebastian nodded, pulling it out of his pocket. "I've only got one left." He checked to see that the glowing purple potion bulb was chambered and ready.

"Well then, you'd better not miss," Ellis cautioned. "Dart the guard and get into that office the second he goes down. I'll be right behind you."

Sebastian nodded again. Ellis dropped the shadow goggles onto her face and saw the glow from Sebastian's hush puppy amplify the purple aura of his cloaker. He floated forward like a soap bubble, and when he was near the guard, he delivered a dart into the man's neck. The glowing purple bubble bobbed into the office.

"Ow!" The guard swiped at the chin strap on his helmet, assuming the pinch had come from his equipment. Ellis surged forward, holding her invisibility spell close as she barreled into the office and spun into the near corner. As the guard thumped to the floor, she slammed and locked the office door, then popped back into view.

"Hello, Senator," Ellis greeted, blocking the door. Sebastian popped up by her side, leveling the dart gun at Chan and her aides. They didn't know it was empty.

"Help!" a young woman in a cherry-red blazer screamed, running for the door. Ellis pushed her away with more force than she intended, and the young woman flew into the wall.

"Who the hell are you?" another aide asked.

"A constituent," Ellis drawled. "Although I wouldn't say the senator will get my vote."

"Ellis," Chan said, somewhere between a hiss and a sigh.

"Not happy to see me?"

"Every time you appear, some new horror descends on the American government."

"You've created plenty of your own horrors," Ellis shot back.

Chan nodded in acknowledgment, then turned to Sebastian, squinting. "I don't think we've been introduced." Her gaze took in the freckles that covered his cheeks like leopard spots.

"This is Sebastian," Ellis clarified. "He's..." Her voice trailed off before she said, "my cousin." "He's a friend."

"Are you two here to kill me?" Chan asked. "Or take me hostage, perhaps? Fool me once…"

"I'm not here to kill you. I'm here to ask for your help," Ellis corrected.

Chan laughed so loudly that her aides leapt back. They exchanged glances, clearly trying to decide if their boss had gone off the deep end. A young man in a khaki blazer snuck a hand into his pocket and pulled out a phone.

"Put that down!" Ellis barked, pointing.

"No one needs to play hero," Chan told the young man. The phone dropped to the floor, and she nodded. "Don't put yourself in danger on my account."

"I don't want anyone getting hurt either," Ellis agreed.

"Is that what you said to the man you sliced in half?" Chan asked.

Ellis winced at the memory of blood under her boots. The violence had been sickening, but even worse had been the current of manic joy the sword had jolted her with when it sliced through body armor and flesh like it was air. That was when she'd truly understood the power of what she had stolen.

"He was shooting a machine gun at me," Ellis protested weakly.

"That's generally what the military does when you try to steal powerful weapons from them."

Chan was right. If you broke into a weapons bunker, someone would try to stop you with guns. "I wasn't just there for the sword. You were holding my friends captive."

"Because they broke into a military bioweapons facility."

The aides looked even more nervous. Ellis was flustered. It was difficult to argue with someone who was being so reasonable. "I had a good reason for breaking into Chiaro. My father was going to die, and I needed their antiviral serum."

"Hah!" Chan exclaimed, a look of triumph on her face. Another nervous current flowed between the aides, and then the senator said, "I knew it was you!"

"Fine. Yes. It was me. Like I said, my father was dying from a virus Marusya Klimova infected him with. I saved your stupid country from her, remember?"

"We can tally up our wins and losses all night," Chan offered. "Or you can tell me why you're here."

"We worked together once before," Ellis clarified. "I'm hoping we can do it again."

"What sort of concessions are you offering?"

This was where things got tricky. "If you help me, I will give back the sword." Shrugging it off her back, she held it before her by the scabbard.

The aides looked curious. Chan's expression was briefly ravenous, then reformed into her impassive political mask. She waved a dismissive hand. "I don't care what the petroglyphs say. It's just a sword. If I want a sword, I'll go to the Renaissance Pleasure Faire and buy one."

Ellis' brain buzzed. What had Chan just said?

"Petroglyphs? What petroglyphs?" Ellis asked. This field trip had been worth it after all.

Chan flinched. She hadn't meant to reveal that. Maybe the sword had tugged it out of her. Chan allowed her gaze to rest on the scabbard. Ellis' fingers tightened on the icy metal. If the senator accepted the deal, could she let the sword go? She would have to force herself to.

"Did you kill my guard?" Chan asked, gaze drifting to the door.

"No. We just disabled him."

"What do you want?" Chan asked.

"You grew up in Los Angeles, right? Lots of friends and family here? I want you to remember that little kerfuffle with Marusya Klimova where I saved your hometown. She's dead, by the way."

"Klimova?"

Ellis nodded. The lines on Chan's face deepened. "I admit I'll sleep easier knowing she's gone for good. Do you have proof?"

"No, but she's our mutual enemy. I have no reason to lie about that."

"You want what, a medal? A pardon?" Chan asked.

Ellis shook her head. "I saved your friends and family. Now I want your help saving mine."

"The big red dot in Angeles National Forest," Chan murmured. "How many drow live there?"

Her tone was curious, but Ellis felt the edge. "I'm sure you'd love to relay my answer to the nearest military attaché. The drow are people just like you. Just like everyone in Los Angeles. They don't trust humans for reasons I'm sure you understand."

A memory of the lightsilk cages in the room the DRI had called "the Zoo" flashed through Ellis' mind. "You tortured my brother, and it still affects him. Some of the drow you held hostage never recovered."

"I didn't do anything," Chan rebutted sharply.

"You could have stopped it, and you didn't," Ellis accused.

The aides gave each other sick looks. Chan looked chagrined. Politics had hardened her shell but hadn't hollowed her out. "I'm very sorry for what happened to your brother and the others. I wasn't aware of the...full scope of activities at the DRI."

"You are now, and that's the kind of horror and violence I'm trying to avoid. If cooler heads don't prevail on both sides, things will get ugly. Humans and drow worked together at the Outpost. We have to find a similar diplomatic solution *now* before it's too late."

"You might have to go above my head for that. I'm not the Commander-in-chief," Chan explained.

"No, you're not, but I bet he'll take your call," Ellis opined.

Chan nodded. "He will, yes. These days, a lot of people in the government are eager to pick my brain about the DRI. May I get my phone?"

"You've got the President on speed dial, huh?"

"Something like that," Chan nodded again.

Ellis watched closely as she stepped toward the desk in the middle of the room and slid open the top drawer.

By the time Ellis saw the confetti gun, it was too late. Chan pulled the trigger, and the room fragmented into shiny shards. The intense overhead lights bounced everywhere. Ellis screamed as the first lightsilk scraps settled on her skin, singeing the hairs on her arms.

The void sword's scabbard vibrated in her hands, and before Ellis realized what she was doing, she had drawn it. The second her fist wrapped around the hilt, an icy wave of power washed through her body under the surface of her skin. As it flowed through her legs and arms, the lightsilk fragments that had settled on her skin froze and crumbled into dust. As quickly as the red welts had risen, they disappeared. More importantly, her shadow senses returned as if someone had pressed the play button.

Sebastian was batting lightsilk off his skin. He wasn't a shadow mage, so the fabric hadn't burned him, although his skin was puffy and red in a few spots.

Chan's hand shook when she saw that, but she leveled the gun at Ellis and shot again.

This time, there was no glittering explosion. The lightsilk poured out of the gun in a stream and flowed into Ellis' black blade. The weapon sucked in the confetti like soda through a straw and vibrated gleefully as the final few scraps disappeared.

Chan depressed the trigger again, but the gun was empty. "What the hell?"

A battering ram slammed into the door. Ellis looked back. "You can call this off." Her sword was still raised, and the senator looked petrified. Her feet were superglued to the floor, and her pupils were huge and black.

"Senator Chan!" Ellis cried.

Chan remained frozen, her eyes fixed on the window.

What the hell is happening?

The room began to darken. It was so subtle that, at first, Ellis thought it was only a change in mood. After a moment, however, she realized the patch of sky framed by the largest window was fading from hazy white to gray. After a moment, it went dark.

The aide in the red blazer reached for her cell phone and checked the time. It was nine A.M., yet the window was a rectangle of midnight darkness. The sun had disappeared.

They gathered around the window, looking at the sky. Smog blocked their view of the stars, which was normal for Los Angeles, although it made the darkness seem even more complete. Had she forgotten about a solar eclipse? Ellis didn't think so.

With great effort, Chan shook off her daze. "What's going on? What did you do?"

"Me?" Ellis asked. "I didn't do anything."

"You pointed that sword at me and turned off the sun!" Chan accused.

Six phones buzzed simultaneously, and the aides' hands reached for their pockets. A muffled voice in the passage warned them to stand back. Then the battering ram hit again, and the door splintered.

Chan wasn't going to help them. After the Chiaro Institute and silo heists, there was too much bad blood between them.

Ellis debated her options. She doubted she'd have much trouble fighting off whoever had busted down the door, but she didn't want any innocent people getting caught in the crossfire. She and Sebastian would go out the back.

"Let's go!" Ellis grabbed her cousin's arm. Shoving Chan aside, she barreled toward the back wall, twirling the void sword in a tall loop. The wall dissolved in front of them, and Ellis pulled Sebastian outside in a quad-burning leap.

They landed hard enough on the patchy lawn to make Ellis' knees ache, but she ignored the pain. Pulling Sebastian with her, she wrapped them both in an invisibility spell and darted between two incoming guards. Fortunately, the sun's disappearance had created chaos outside, and there were plenty of gaps in the crowd surrounding the building. Ellis found the nearest opening and pulled Sebastian across Spring Street into the quiet of a mostly abandoned dog park.

When they were some distance away, Ellis pulled Sebastian behind a tree. "Do you know what she meant by 'petroglyphs?'" Ellis asked.

He was looking at the dark sky and didn't answer. When she tugged on his arm and repeated the question, he blinked in confusion. "No. I don't know anything." Sebastian shivered. "What's happening?"

It was a good question. The sky had been black for long enough to rule out a solar eclipse. The city was still dark, and few of the buildings had turned on their exterior lights. Los Angeles had never looked deader.

"Was Chan right?" Sebastian asked. "Did *you* do this with the sword?" He inched away from the naked blade.

Seeing his fear, Ellis slid it back into the scabbard. "I didn't have anything to do with it." *At least, I hope not.* Ellis' phone buzzed. When she checked it, she found a text from her father.

Meet me at the oak knot bolthole

"Dad wants us to meet him."

"Do you think he'll know what's going on?" Sebastian asked. His eyes were shadowed in the dark park.

"Maybe." She wasn't sure. "Let's find out."

The oak knot bolthole would have been easy to get to under normal circumstances, but the police had blocked off Highway 2 above La Cañada, and their detour took ages. The sky was still dark, although now that they were in the forest, the smog had cleared enough for the stars to reappear.

It was comforting to know that the Earth had hurtled into a magical void. By the time they arrived at their destination, little more than a shallow supply cache, they were starving. Sebastian dug through the bolthole's contents and handed her a tunnel bar. They ate in silence.

Half an hour later, Connor strode through the bushes. "Are you all right?"

"I've been better. Where's Percy?" Ellis asked.

"Sitting inside a hollow log communing with the animals. I tried to bring him with me, but he wouldn't leave."

"Is he okay?" Ellis asked.

"Physically? Hm. Yes."

Ellis told him about their meeting with Chan.

"I'd hoped she would be an ally. At heart, I believe she's a rational person," Connor mused.

"Nothing is rational anymore. The fucking sun is gone," Ellis snapped. Just then, she noticed that the moon, which should have been waxing, was also dark. "Have you been to the Homestead?"

"No. They caved in the main entrance as a defensive measure. I haven't found a way in yet."

"Shit. Do you know what's going on? Why it got dark at nine in the morning and stayed that way?"

Connor was silent for a long time, so he knew something.

"What? What is it?"

He sank down and wrapped his arms around his knees. "It's the first of the three omens."

Sebastian looked at Ellis to explain this pronouncement, but she was in the dark too. Nearby, a small animal moved through the bushes. "Are you going to tell us what you know or just stare ominously at the forest?" Ellis asked.

Connor looked up. "I thought the spell was apocryphal."

Ellis crossed her arms and glared at him. "What spell?"

Finally, he sighed. "Your nan told me about the three omens when I was little. I thought the story was a fairytale to scare children."

"You never passed it along to me. I don't remember any scary stories."

"There was no point. You were never scared of anything," Connor smiled faintly. Sebastian hoovered up knowledge about the grandmother he'd never known.

"According to the story, the drow elders had a secret weapon they could draw on in times of crisis." Ellis glanced at the void sword, but Connor shook his head. "Not a sword. Something bigger and more dangerous."

Ellis' eyebrows crept up. The sword was plenty dangerous. "What, a bomb or something?"

"No, a creature. A gift of the Mother Beneath. Something wild and dangerous that would protect the drow if all other defenses failed."

"Okay. So, some big cave dragon monster stumbled out of the ground and ate the sun?"

"Not exactly. Summoning the creature requires a massive amount of magical effort. It requires three rituals, and each is accompanied by an omen."

"And this is the first omen?" Ellis stared at the cold, dark moon. The starlight also filled her with unease.

"Yes. The darkness is a warning."

"To humans?" Ellis asked curiously.

"To some extent, yes. Total darkness makes it easier for the drow to work shadow magic. It is also a warning to the drow. An indication of the seriousness of the summoning."

"The sun's not actually gone, is it?" Ellis wasn't equipped for nuclear winter.

"No. It's blocked by a magical occlusion. It's ancient magic, and I do not understand how it works. It is possible that no one does." Connor turned to Sebastian. "In all your travels and communications, have any drow mentioned something like that to you? A monster or creature made of darkness?"

"No. Not one. We would have tried to find it."

"The monster?" Ellis asked.

"Mostly, the *Violet Eel* hunted monsters of the human variety, but we would have looked, yeah. Or at least tried to find more information."

Ellis hated this. She liked her weapons simple and easy to wield. A shiver from the metal scabbard on her back reminded her that the void sword was neither.

Connor's face was dark and troubled as he continued, "Human military forces are massing at the western edge of the forest, and Percy says the entire food chain is on high alert. The animals keep feeding him rumors of scouts—humans, not drow—traipsing through the woods, looking for signs of the Homestead."

"This qualifies as a serious emergency. Maybe…maybe it isn't so bad for the drow to summon a shadow monster.

It's possible we'll need supernatural help to stave off the humans. Right?"

Connor's frown deepened as he leaned back into a patch of purple-black shadows. "The stories Nan told me about the creature…" Ellis and Sebastian leaned forward. "They were not heroic. They were not noble accounts of desperate triumph over insurmountable human forces."

"What were they, then?"

"Cautionary tales. In one story, a powerful drow magician summoned the creature after a trade dispute with a human village."

"A *trade* dispute? That must be a very old story." It had been hundreds of years since drow and humans had openly traded.

"Very old," Connor agreed. "Anyway, in the tale, the magician refuses help from the other drow. He wants to prove how strong and powerful he is, but though he is strong enough to summon the monster, he is not strong enough to control it. The creature breaks free from its magical chains. It eats him, then devours the human village, children and all. The magician dies, and his community loses their best magician and a valuable trade partner. Men with steel come asking questions, and the drow have to move deeper into the forest."

"Oh," Ellis muttered. "But that was just a story. Maybe it wasn't a warning. Maybe Nan Elandra didn't know the creature was real."

"It's possible, although she was a wise woman with a long memory. Still, whoever first told that tale was relaying an important message."

"Don't go summoning shadow monsters willy-nilly," Ellis tried to make it a joke, but no one laughed.

"Exactly."

"Who do you think is performing the summoning ritual?" Ellis asked. "Could it be a drow community on the other side of the Earth? That would present a less immediate problem."

Connor shook his head. "The darkness is local. It must be the drow elders in the Homestead since they're the only ones with that kind of power. After Lola's coup, they're on edge. I doubt they want to risk negotiating with the humans."

There was a strange cry from the forest. Patchy clouds had blown in, blocking half the stars. During eclipses, animals behaved strangely. The sudden twilight threw off their routines. Spiders took down their webs, and confused vultures settled in to roost in the middle of the day. Percy was undoubtedly hearing strange things from the local wildlife. What would they do if the sky stayed dark for days or even weeks? "Is it reversible?"

"What do you mean?"

"You said the ritual had three steps, each accompanied by an omen. This is step number one, right?" Ellis glanced at the sky. "Does something bad happen if the shadow mages performing the ritual just *stop*?"

Connor shook his head. "Fairytales aren't instruction manuals. I'd guess that if they stop, the shadow magic will eventually disperse."

"I'm not sure they should stop," Sebastian murmured.

Connor raised an eyebrow. Given his history, Ellis

knew where Sebastian was coming from. "A pre-emptive offense might be better than defense," Sebastian continued. "The US military has *nukes,* fer chrissake."

"The government isn't going to drop nukes on its second-largest city." Ellis scoffed. "The citizens would revolt."

"The citizens might demand it if they got scared enough," Sebastian countered.

When Charlie had learned that Ellis could dissolve physical objects with her magic, he'd been horrified. So horrified that he had struggled to do that magic himself. His mind had rebelled, and Charlie liked her. Possibly even loved her.

Even when he understood how shadow magic worked on a deep and personal level, he had remained frightened, and humans as a species had little of Charlie's goodwill toward the drow. There was no telling what they or their government might do.

She imagined a colossal magical monster with matte-black scales and violet eyes swirling with shadow magic. Maybe a cross between an elephant and an angry column of smoke. She imagined it chewing through a picnic at Griffith Park, swallowing the Hollywood Sign, and leaving the brass stars in front of the Chinese Theater wet with blood.

Ellis liked Los Angeles and its people enough that she didn't want to see them consumed by an abyssal beast. "No. We can't let this happen."

"I don't want any drow communities destroyed. It's my fault that this has gotten out of hand, and we can't ask them not to defend themselves," Sebastian offered.

"We won't," Ellis countered. "The gap between 'defenseless' and 'protected by a magical monster' is wide enough to sail a ship through."

Sebastian flinched at the mention of ships.

"Perhaps the drow will reconsider their course of action," Connor added. "The darkness might be enough to scare the humans out of hitting us."

They all looked at the sky. Ellis blinked. While they had been speaking, the stars had disappeared. In their place, thick thunderheads had massed. The weather had turned quickly. Too quickly.

The nearest cloud flashed purple.

"What is that?" Ellis asked. She had lived her whole life with magic, but she had never seen anything like the violet light illuminating those clouds.

As Connor opened his mouth to speak, a bright purple bolt hit a tree a hundred feet away in the forest. Rather than be absorbed, the bolt ricocheted back up into the clouds, forking into jagged tentacles that pierced the sky. Before anyone could speak, a crack of thunder like the swansong of a dying god filled the negative space between the trees, pressing against her skin and eyes. She slapped her hands over her ears, but the noise dug spikes of pain into her eardrums.

"*What is that?*" Ellis demanded as the lightning flashed again. The purple light turned her skin the lilac color she'd always craved, but only for a moment. This time, she clapped her hands over her ears before the thunder hit.

"That's the second omen," Connor explained. Ellis' ears were ringing, so her father had to shout to be heard.

"They're moving fast! We have to get to the Homestead and stop them."

"What if we can't find an entrance?" Ellis asked.

"Then we'll have to make one."

CHAPTER EIGHT

Luckily, they didn't have to drill blindly into the strata above the Homestead. The first five entrances they tried had been caved in, but after nearly a full day, they found one that was still clear—one of Connor's secret emergency exits, nestled behind a boulder near an old mining cabin two miles up a trail.

It stormed the whole time, which made the search terrifying. The magical clouds produced no rain but discharged regular lightning that dissolved the tops of nearby trees and, in one case, sent a slab of sandstone sliding off a cliff. When they finally climbed into the mouth of the tunnel, it was a relief to put rock between them and the storm.

Ellis wished they could spend a few minutes recovering, but there wasn't enough room in the tunnel to stand up straight, much less relax. Still, getting out of the intense purple lightning provided a degree of relaxation, even as their hunched bodies shuffled down a gentle slope. Even when they reached the main tunnel, there was little time for rest. Ellis and Connor used shadow magic to keep themselves invisible, and Sebastian flicked on his cloaker.

Sebastian was excited to be in the Homestead. He had never visited his grandmother's home, and was animated by boyish enthusiasm. He looked around alertly, running his hands across the magically chiseled-out walls and inspecting the floor.

"The construction's good. It won't cave in on us," Ellis assured him.

Sebastian smiled. "I'm not worried about that. I've been in a dozen drow homesteads, and every one is different. The style here is very…functional. It's curious. This is one of the larger drow communities, but the decorations carved into the rock are minimal.

"There are places where it's more elaborate." Ellis sounded defensive. She didn't want the Swallow's Nest compared unfavorably to other homesteads.

"It's not a criticism. Just a difference. Every homestead is a new adventure," Sebastian told her. There was genuine enthusiasm in his eyes. For all his flaws, Sebastian loved the drow. He had dedicated his life to doing what he thought was best for them, even if his judgment had occasionally been questionable.

"They're sort of a mixed bag when it comes to half-drow," Ellis continued. "They're coming around, but don't expect a parade."

"I understand," Sebastian replied. Ellis was used to people telling her they understood what she was going through. Sebastian, who had also grown up with a foot in another world, really *did*. She was glad her cousin had come into her life.

"Let's go straight to the elders," Connor suggested. "I have a good rapport with them. They'll know what's going on, and I might be able to convince them to stop."

It took a long time to make their way through the tunnels. Lola's coup had taken its toll on the physical structures of the Homestead, although it was hard to tell which tunnels had been damaged by the fighting and which had been collapsed as a defensive measure against human incursion. Only stragglers remained in the outlying tunnels, and Ellis wondered if most of the community had evacuated.

The crowds got denser when they passed the inner ring tunnel. Instead of evacuating, the drow had congregated in the Homestead's central areas. It became difficult to avoid the crush of bodies, and they moved at a cave-slug's pace.

The Speakers' Chamber had caved in during Lola's coup, so the elders had commandeered the mushroom caverns as an alternative meeting place. As they approached, Ellis' heart rose into her throat. She hoped the mushroom caverns hadn't been damaged in the coup. She envisioned smoking rows of morels and portobellos, her careful cultivations ripped from their growth medium and stomped to pieces.

The familiar smell as they stepped through the arch into the caverns dispelled Ellis' fears. The wholesome decay and earthy undertones told her the caverns were still in good shape.

Connor and Sebastian made a beeline to the elders, but Ellis couldn't help but detour along the cavern's perimeter, slipping a green morel into her pocket and harvesting a massive portobello. She tested the springiness of its hamburger-sized cap before taking a large bite. Whatever else had happened during the troubles, the drow hadn't let it destroy the quality of their fungiculture. Pride surged through Ellis as she rejoined the others.

Only four elders were in the cavern.

"Where are the others?" Ellis asked. Katya shook her head sadly, and a wave of sorrow washed over Ellis. Not all of them had made it through the coup, and it wasn't just the elders' numbers that were diminished. Each seemed to have shrunk, recent events sucking the life from their deflated bodies.

Katya looked as exhausted as the rest, but there was something different about her. A resolute hardness, as if the recent crises had revealed her underlying steel. Even bent over her metal staff, she was formidable.

Banging her staff on the rock floor below the growth medium, Katya straightened, the crack of her old bones echoing through the cavern. She looked Sebastian up and down. "Yes. I can see the familial resemblance around the eyes. Hah. Even dead, Elandra still has a few surprises up her sleeve."

"You didn't know about me?" Sebastian asked.

Katya shook her head. "When Elandra and I were young, relationships between humans and drow were a bit looser. Not loose enough for a human child to fit in, though."

Some things never change. "I wish I had known her," Sebastian murmured.

"I wish she had known you," Katya replied. "She might have beat some of your fool ideas out of your thick skull." Sebastian winced, but Katya plowed ahead. "Because of your actions, human warriors are bearing down on the Swallow's Nest. In days gone by, we might have called on another homestead for aid, but you've made quite sure that they're all too busy to help."

"I'm sorry. I didn't plan for things to happen like this," Sebastian pleaded.

"Actually, you did," Ellis stated angrily. "This is exactly what you planned. You just didn't have the guts to pull the trigger."

Sebastian's freckles darkened. However, arguing about his culpability wouldn't change anything, and he shrugged. "What are you going to do now?"

"About you, or about the humans at our door?" Katya asked, one silver eyebrow rising.

"Both."

"Well, conveniently for you, we're a bit busy for recriminations. As for the human crisis…" Her gaze settled on Connor, and she planted her metal staff. "Connor, we would like your help to finish the summoning."

"No," Ellis said flatly. "The summoning is a bad idea. You have to stop! We came here to put an end to this."

"I didn't ask for your opinion, child," Katya snapped. She looked Ellis over. "You've gotten your shadow magic back."

"Not completely. I'm still reliant on a special mushroom potion. How did you know?" Ellis asked.

"I'm the most powerful shadow mage in this warren, and I've been around for a long time."

"I have Dad and Trissa to thank for the potion," Ellis relayed.

"You were always a skilled shadow mage. It made a

strong argument for more interactions with humans. Although it's not a straight line. You haven't got any magic," Katya informed Sebastian.

The intended insult slid off him. Ellis remained amazed by how non-defensive he was about his total lack of shadow magic. She would have liked to have known his mother, she realized. "I have other skills," Sebastian asserted.

"You have a big mouth is what you have. And a bigger ego." Katya poked Sebastian in the chest with her staff.

"I care about the drow. I'm fighting for their future," Sebastian shot back. "You can't stay troglodytes forever."

"Not anymore, we can't." Katya sighed. "You made sure of that. Well, stay out of our way, boy. We'll deal with you later. Ellis, we would welcome your help with the summoning. We *must* have a weapon to wield against the humans."

"No."

"It's madness," Connor agreed.

"We're going to forge ahead, with or without you," Katya asserted.

Connor rubbed his forehead. "Surely you've heard the stories about the kind of destruction the monster could wreak."

"Against humans, not drow," Katya countered.

"The humans outnumber us, Elder Speaker." Connor's voice was very formal. He opened his hands in supplication. "Releasing a monster against them will only make them angry and harden them against a diplomatic solution. Our best chance of survival lies in cooperation."

"Humans don't know how to cooperate. They only know how to destroy," Katya growled.

"That's not true," Ellis argued.

"Oh? Look at your mother. Your father cooperated with her." The blow opened an old wound, and both Ellis and Connor winced. Ellis knew in her heart that there was more to humans than blind violence. She had seen it in Percy, and Charlie, and Rose.

"Drow are capable of just as much hatred as humans. Believe me, I know," Ellis stated icily. When Katya didn't take the bait, she added, "Lola caused more harm to this place than humans ever have."

At that, Katya was silent. Then, she slammed her staff on the ground three times. It speared through the mushroom growth medium and clanged on the stone. When she spoke, there was a fire in her eyes. "This was an invitation to help, not argue. If you won't aid your people in their time of need, so be it."

"We won't help you summon a monster," Ellis agreed.

"Ellis," Connor murmured. She turned to him, expecting him to come forward with a new argument. An angle of attack to sway Katya that they hadn't thought of. Instead, his face was sad. He swiveled slowly toward the elder speaker.

"I will aid you," he confirmed, his voice a low rumble.

Ellis sucked in her breath at the betrayal. "Dad, no! You can't!"

He was going to help the elders. "You remember the story I told you? The weapon is safer when more hands wield it. I can help control the monster. Stop the worst from happening…if it comes to that."

Katya wasn't thrilled about his pronouncement, but she wouldn't look a gift horse in the mouth. "One last time. Will you join us?" she asked Ellis.

Ellis shook her head. "I'm going to warn Percy. Make sure he's weathering the storm okay, and maybe convince him to leave. He is human."

Katya nodded. "I bear your friend no ill will."

"I'd like to stay here and watch," Sebastian requested. "Gather information about the summoning ritual."

Katya snorted. "We will not share our deepest secrets with a non-magical outsider." Sebastian seemed less personally offended than disappointed about not getting to observe a new facet of drow culture.

"You can come with me," Ellis offered. "I would welcome the company."

CHAPTER NINE

It took Ellis a while to find the hollow log Percy had hunkered down in. Purple lightning hit the canopy above them at random, rattling the pines and making Ellis' blue-black hair stand on end. Between earsplitting cracks of thunder, she raised her hands above her head and clapped. The animals of the forest were spooked and silent, and no squirrel or deer or crow appeared as a guide.

She and Sebastian had wrapped lengths of crystal silk around their heads to protect their hearing. Deadening one of their senses left them vulnerable, but it was better than having their eardrums blown out by magical thunder.

As they ascended the side of a small ravine, a crack of lightning hit a nearby tree, which toppled into their path. Ellis and Sebastian scrambled away, barely avoiding being skewered by the falling branches. The crash dislodged a number of small birds, who chirped anxiously as they scattered.

Taking this opportunity, Ellis hopped onto a nearby rock, raised her hands, and clapped three times. One of the songbirds made a small circle in the air, inspecting her, and Ellis repeated the motion. The bird chirped and flew away.

A few minutes later, a bedraggled squirrel climbed to the top of a rock at the edge of the ravine and chittered at them, puffing out its chest. Ellis pointed the squirrel out to Sebastian. "We've got our forest guide." The squirrel bravely led them through the storm to a small hollow beneath a fallen tree, surrounded by bundled scrub. Percy was barely visible in the back, scrunched into a ball with his arms around his legs.

"Percy," Ellis called. When he leaned into the light, Ellis gasped. He'd never looked so haggard. There were bruised violet half-moons under his eyes, and he was jumpier than normal. He waved them forward, then went back to picking pine needles off a dry branch one by one.

Lightning flashed in the sky, and Ellis winced. Even through the crystal silk, the thunder's crack was punishing. Percy didn't even bother to cover his ears, which worried her. When the noise had quieted, she grabbed his arm.

"Come on," Ellis called, probably too loudly. Percy barely seemed to hear her but allowed her to pull him closer. Casting a reluctant look at the sky, Ellis unwound the crystal silk from her head. "What's wrong?"

There was another low rumble of thunder, fortunately distant. Percy stared at her blankly. "The animals are going crazy. They're used to storms, a'course, but not purple lightning, and not this thunder. It's loud enough to knock songbirds outta the sky. The noise is unbearable."

There was more lighting, and Ellis put her hands over her ears. When Percy didn't bother, Ellis realized that he wasn't talking about the noise from the thunder. He was talking about the psychic noise from the ecosystem. A forest full of terrified animals screaming into his brain. The humans and drow had some grasp of why everything was upside-down. The animals had no such luck.

Ellis made Percy drink some water, then handed him a tunnel bar. "Here. Fresh off the presses."

"Thanks." Percy chewed quietly, although when the thunder cracked, he stopped, eyes and mind elsewhere.

Ellis told Percy what her father had decided. He pressed his lips together.

"Do you think you'll be able to talk to the monster?" Ellis asked. Was a monster an animal? She wasn't sure, and apparently, neither was he.

"I can try if things get bad. Or even if they don't. It's always nice to make new friends." Only Percy would immediately assume that a shadow magic monster might make a good friend.

It took an interminably long time, but Percy finally finished eating the tunnel bar. Ellis made him drink more water.

"I wish they'd let me stay for the summoning," Sebastian muttered in the silence.

"Why?" Ellis asked.

"Because it's interesting," Sebastian stated. "I've tried to learn as much about drow magic as I can."

Ellis wondered why he would bother. He couldn't cast it, so why would he want to see it? Maybe, with the shadow goggles, it was interesting to watch.

"If the drow create a shadow monster that eats everyone alive, It won't be *interesting*," Ellis countered.

"Speak for yourself," Sebastian shot back.

"If it comes to that, we'll try to stop it." The void sword gave an enthusiastic pulse.

"We should have asked your father about the third omen," Sebastian continued.

He was right. The first and second omens had been impossible to miss, but it would be nice to be prepared. She realized she was expecting the geologic layers at their feet to rise like a punched cake as the creature crawled out of the Earth. She imagined it dormant in a cave, opening its eyes as her father and the elders completed the summoning.

Maybe that was wrong. Maybe the monster wasn't like that. Wasn't waiting. Maybe they were making it out of thin air.

Maybe the third omen wouldn't be so extreme. What if she missed it? What if it was subtle, a shadow across the moon or something like that?

As it turned out, her fear was groundless. The third omen was as subtle as a slap, although there was no earthquake. The ground beneath their feet did not rebel. The lightning in the sky got more infrequent, then stopped. They were all sitting quietly in the hollow, in nervous anticipation of what was to come, when Percy screamed at the top of his lungs.

"What is it?" Ellis asked. Percy was insensible to the question, his wails drowning out her voice. His screams got louder between hacking too-fast breaths. He had his hands on his temples, fingers spread across his scalp.

"What's wrong? Are you injured?" Ellis asked. She saw no wounds on his body, but he was clearly in immense distress.

Something hit Ellis on the head. *Hail?* She raised her hand to her scalp and touched something firm and slick. When she pulled it down to inspect it, she found that it was a fish. Small and very dead, its silver body inert in her hand. She looked at Sebastian in alarm and saw a massive salmon plummet from the sky, missing him by inches.

"Oh, shit!" Ellis exclaimed.

"The third omen," Sebastian murmured.

The forest, previously quiet, filled with squelching slaps. Silver bodies of all sizes filled the air, some falling to the ground and others ricocheting off tree branches. Before she could say anything else, Sebastian grabbed her arm and pulled her deeper into the hollow, under the cover of the tree. Percy's keening had quieted to a low sob, and as more fish fell, Ellis understood.

Ellis didn't like to see animals injured. She ate meat, though, and it was hard for her to get worked up about fish. For Percy, hearing thousands of terrified animals fall from the sky must have been excruciating. He was raking his fingers across his head, trying to cover his skull with his hands.

"It's okay," Ellis urged, though it wasn't. The rain of fish was horrible. Ellis scooched to the edge of the overhang and peered through the brush. Another fish hit her arm and slid off into a bush. She reached down to dig it out when another one hit. This time, she caught it in her palm.

It was a thin-bodied fish a few inches long, the kind of silver thread that caught the light in shallow, stagnant water. Ellis peered into the sky and saw a massive carp plummeting toward her head. She pulled her head back under the overhang with a yelp.

No wonder Percy was disconsolate. He could control his animal psychic powers to some extent, but the fish must have been in serious pain, and the downpour wasn't waning. He'd said before that fish were simple creatures. Pain and death were simple, too. The flood of anguished creatures had clearly broken his psychic defenses.

Sebastian was sitting near Percy, careful not to touch him. Ellis pushed her cousin aside and wrapped her arm around Percy's shoulder. "I'm so sorry, Perce," she murmured, squeezing him. His howling got quieter, but he didn't acknowledge her presence. All she could do was be there with him while they waited.

No one spoke again until several minutes after the silver downpour stopped. The shower didn't last long — maybe ten minutes—but it left them all depleted. Percy remained practically catatonic until the nearby vegetation rustled and footsteps approached. Exhausted, Ellis got to her feet, sword in hand. She relaxed when her father stepped out from behind a tree. His foot landed on a trout, and he nearly lost his balance.

"You're all still here." Connor grabbed a tree branch to haul himself upright.

"I gather the summoning was successful," Ellis snarled.

Face grim, Connor nodded. "The beast will appear at sunrise. We'll know then, I guess, although the third omen was strong and clear."

"*You bastard!*" Percy exploded out of the hollow. Animated by raw rage, he punched Connor in the chest. That didn't appear to hurt the drow, although he looked surprised. "*You killed them,*" Percy screamed.

Connor looked confused until Ellis explained, "He means the fish."

"I'm sorry." Connor's face was pale and still. "I did not think about how the third omen would affect you."

"Don't apologize to me," Percy screamed. *"Apologize to them."* He gestured around. "How would you like it if I flung you out of a plane as some kind of fish portent?" He took a half-step back as if winding up for another blow. But when he sprang forward, it was only to push Connor aside. Dancing between the fallen silver bodies, he made his way into the forest. Ellis tried to follow him but slammed her head into a low-hanging branch. By the time she had recovered, Percy had disappeared.

"Should we go after him?" Sebastian asked.

"Perhaps." Connor sighed. "I came to bring you back to the Homestead. We got word from the rangers. An Army battalion is marching toward the main entrance."

"It's collapsed though, right?" Ellis asked.

"It is, yes, but they appear to have brought mining equipment."

"That's not good," Ellis muttered.

"No. We should return to the Homestead while we wait for the summoning to work."

"We have to find Percy first," Ellis argued. Her friend was in immense pain, and she wouldn't leave him behind.

"He might be safer with the animals than he is with us," Connor told her.

Ellis ignored him and headed into the forest. The fallen fish were dull gray in the moonlight, and stepping across—and by necessity on top of—their fallen bodies was dangerous and unpleasant. Muddy footsteps told her that

Percy had headed down a game trail, but as Ellis moved in that direction, a large black animal stepped onto the trail.

At first, Ellis thought it was the shadow monster. The animal let out a low wuffle, and as Ellis reached for the hilt of the void blade, it stepped into a patch of moonlight.

It was a black bear. With half a salmon dangling from its mouth, it did not look threatening. It looked ebullient, like a small child in a bathtub full of Sour Patch Kids. When Ellis took a half-step toward it, it growled and swiped at the air, not wanting its pescatarian bacchanal interrupted.

The bear's posture made Ellis think this wasn't a random encounter. Every so often, its dark eyes lost focus as if it were listening to a far-off noise. The expression was familiar.

"Percy doesn't want us following him," Ellis told her party, backing away. The bear sat on its haunches and pawed through the selection of fish within reach, settling for a perch.

"Is Percy likely to run smack-dab into a military patrol?" Sebastian asked.

Ellis didn't think so. "The animals will let him know before that happens."

"Is he likely to turn his coat?" Sebastian asked.

"No!" Ellis exclaimed immediately after he finished the question. Percy might be angry, but he wouldn't betray them.

The bear scratched the trail, leaving deep gouges. He looked eager to get back to his sushi dinner. "Then leave him be," Sebastian suggested. "Let's go see what we can do for the Homestead."

"We'll ask the rangers to keep an eye out for him," Connor told his daughter.

Before Ellis went into the caves, she called Charlie. Her heart skipped a beat when he answered the phone. "What's going on?" he asked. There was a lot of noise in the background.

Ellis wanted to tell him everything, but she was afraid. What if he told the LAPD about the monster? Maybe that would be better. At the very least, they could evacuate civilians from the area.

"This is a mess," Ellis began. The drow were vulnerable, and they were acting out of fear. That made them dangerous. Telling Charlie they were about to sic an ancient monster on the humans might not do much to calm tensions. A diplomatic solution was slipping out of her fingers. She hoped she could convince the drow not to release the beast.

"What are the drow up to?" Charlie asked.

Last chance to tell him the truth.

"Battening down the hatches. Preparing defenses." That was true.

"All right. I'm going to see what I can do on my end. Win hearts and minds." Charlie sighed. After a pause, "I love you." It nearly broke Ellis' heart.

"I'll see you soon," she replied.

"Sure." Charlie sounded disappointed. Feeling uneasy, Ellis headed underground.

CHAPTER TEN

Back at the Homestead, Ellis, Connor, and Sebastian gathered in their assigned quarters to talk strategy. Sebastian had plenty to offer in the military intelligence department. The *Violet Eel* had maintained up-to-date information about the fighting capacity of the most significant divisions. Additionally, invisibility was invaluable for reconnaissance. The drow had sent several rangers to keep tabs on the military.

"How much lightsilk do they have?" Ellis asked after her father returned from an update from a messenger.

"Some. They have nets, and we've seen a few confetti guns and ribbons. They don't have enough to blanket the forest looking for us." Ellis wondered how long that would be true. Her father smiled. "In a stroke of good luck, the fish rain grounded their helicopters."

"The pilots must have been very surprised," Sebastian muttered.

"So, what do we do?" Ellis asked.

"We get some sleep and wait for the Mother Beneath to send us her guardian." Connor shrugged.

"That's what you call it? A guardian?"

"That is what Katya says it is," Connor explained.

It took Ellis a long time to fall asleep. The elders didn't know exactly where—or how—the monster would appear, so every time she turned over on the cot in the mushroom caverns, she feared that a many-legged terror would rush toward her out of the darkness, jaws dripping and hungry.

Exhaustion won out in the end. It was not a gentle descent into sleep. The darkness behind her eyes swirled with purple streaks, and she was falling through a familiar dense shadow magic mist. The dream was tactile, the magic cool and moist on her skin.

The dream echoed the vision she'd seen the first time she'd worn the black pearl ring. She had fallen through the mist for what seemed like ages. This time, when a stone platform appeared below her, she was not surprised. The stone was the same brilliant white as before, but this time, there was no reflecting pool.

When her feet touched the rock, gravity resumed its pull. After she regained her balance, Ellis circled the perimeter of the disc. She was looking for something, although she didn't remember what. When she was halfway around, she saw a white stone a foot wide, orbiting the platform like a moon. When Ellis stepped onto the stone, another appeared, then another and another. A long line of stepping stones led into the distance. Ellis skipped lightly across them, not afraid of falling.

The destination was a dark break in the mist, like the mouth of a cave. Ellis ran to it and stepped inside. White stone rose around her as she walked, rough-hewn and low-ceilinged. The low tunnel opened into a broad cavern, and she recognized the statue in the center, a hooded figure. The last time she'd seen it, it had been holding a sword. *Her* sword. This time, the statue was holding an ancient scroll wrapped in crystal silk twine in an open palm.

"Is this for me?" Ellis asked, stepping up to the statue. Long, thin mushrooms on the ceiling above the statue glowed like a halo. Ellis glanced at them, not recognizing the species. *That's because this is a dream, dummy.*

"Hello? Can you hear me?" Ellis called.

The statue didn't answer, so she gently took the scroll from its hand and unwrapped the twine. When she unfurled the parchment, her vision swam. She saw writing, but she could not read it. The golden mushrooms glowed brighter, but the scroll stayed blurred. Ellis' eyes watered in desperation.

"What do you want?" she asked the statue. Its face was dark beneath its hood.

You couldn't read a scroll in a dream any more than you could read tomorrow's newspaper. The blurriness of the words on the parchment started bleeding out toward the cavern's walls and the haloing mushrooms and onto the statue. Everything was blending together, a nightmare of gray soup.

Ellis realized she was waking up. She made one final, desperate attempt to read the scroll, blinking rapidly.

After the final blink, she was staring at the ceiling of the mushroom caverns. Ellis sat up, looking around in alarm to see if she was sharing her quarters with a newborn monster. All she saw were other drow on cots, most asleep.

Ellis chewed on a tunnel bar. They were still waiting for the world to end. That quickly became intolerable, and she went to find her father in his office. Instead, she discovered a young drow man inventorying Connor's potion supplies. "Where's my dad?"

"He already went up top," he conveyed. "With the rest of the elders."

Whatever happened today, she didn't want to be alone, so she packed a satchel with food, water, and the last of her shadow magic potion and followed some rangers into the forest. There, she found her father and the other drow elders gathered in a shallow, grassy basin, drinking mushroom tea and speaking to one another in low voices. The forest floor was still covered in fish, which were beginning to rot. When Ellis joined them, her father offered her a jar of salve.

"For the smell," he explained. She gratefully accepted it, rubbing the greasy fungal ointment into her nostrils. The air was still fishy, but the odor no longer made her want to stuff red-hot pokers in her nostrils. Ellis settled onto a log to watch the sunrise, hoping a morning breeze might bring further relief. It had been a very long night.

The hazy sky remained an undifferentiated dark mass for a long time. When the sun finally cleared the horizon, lightening the sky to gray, it was a relief. Ellis might be a night owl, but she didn't want a world with endless night.

Below the trees, the forest was untouched by the thin

sunlight. Ellis was so focused on the dawn that it took her several minutes to notice the changes in the shadows dappling the undergrowth.

She realized that her feet were cold and saw that the toes of her boots were covered by a dense black fog. When she reached down to touch it, the fog slipped away from her fingers, although it sent an icy chill up her arm.

"It's starting." Connor was pulling shadow magic into his hands.

The fog crept along the ground, flowing down gullies and eddying behind trees, slow and viscous. Ellis climbed atop a fallen log. The black miasma was collecting in the basin. At first it was formless, filling the hollow like water and growing denser.

Then the mist moved.

This had to be the monster.

Ellis scrambled away, her throat tight with primal fear as she fled the hollow. The black mist thickened into an amorphous blob. A nub protruded from the side and lengthened into a tendril that probed the air. Where the dark mass touched, the forest returned to night. The few birds that had chirped nervously when the sun rose fell silent as the darkness touched them.

More tendrils stretched out from the black fog, taking shape like a sculptor's clay, the ends flattening into clubs. Then the bulk of the shadows shot into the air, supported by two trunk-like lumps that had split like tree branches into wide feet.

More tendrils extended from the head—a whole forest of them. Ellis thought those might turn into arms, but they stopped growing when they were only a few feet long, each stalk ending in a bulbous sphere. *What the hell are those?*

She got her answer when several of the bulbs looked at her.

It was all Ellis could do not to sprint away.

The monster had no eyes, not exactly. Its entire surface was a dense black, but when she moved, the bulbous stalk moved with her, tracking her steps across the forest floor. She felt watched.

Then, it emitted a low rumble that rose into a tectonic screech. This was what an earthquake would sound like if it wanted to eat you, Ellis thought. The bulbous stalks turned toward her as the monster howled, and Ellis caught a glimpse inside its open mouth. The sucking maw was full of quivering teeth, obsidian-black and pointed like arrowheads, continuously moving in shifting circles. Ellis heard screams, and it took her a moment to realize they were coming from her mouth.

Scrambling back, limbs no longer under her full control, Ellis slammed into a body. Warm hands gripped her shoulders, and her father's face swam into her vision.

"You should run," he told her and pushed her behind him. At that protective gesture, Ellis' sanity returned.

Connor was spinning a roiling mass of shadow magic between his hands. It was a dangerous amount of magic, although less dangerous than the monster. He stepped forward, chanting in a low voice, and spun a thick rope of magic toward the creature.

The monster had reached its full size, although some of its limbs were still growing.

Later, Ellis had difficulty describing it. The monster

had that quality normally reserved for nightmares, where it shifted in your peripheral vision, morphing into something more fearful each time you looked over your shoulder. It had either four or six limbs, except when it reared onto two legs and walked like that. Its body sometimes stretched out like a snake's.

Ellis wondered if she would be able to feel anything if she touched the monster's skin. Maybe her hand would plunge into black mist. Maybe the mist would be caustic, and she'd pull back a stump.

She wasn't willing to find out.

"Holy shit," someone muttered behind her. Ellis turned to find Sebastian holding up his phone to film the monster. He looked terrified.

"What are you doing?" Ellis growled.

"Research. I've never seen anything like it."

Their conversation was cut off by a scream when the rope of magic streaming from her father's hands touched the creature's nearest limb. Teeth flashed in the wide mouth, and Ellis shuddered. As the swirling magical cord twined around its leg—or trunk, or tentacle, or whatever— the monster's body solidified. It stopped shifting, locked in place by her father's containment spell.

"What *is* that?" Ellis asked, pointing at the cord running from Connor's hands to the monster.

There was movement in the trees behind the monster. Katya emerged opposite Connor. She leaned on her staff with one hand and reached toward the monster with the other. A matching magical rope flowed from her hand and looped around the creature's opposing foot —or arm, or front tail, or whatever the hell you wanted to call it. The other three elders fanned out, casting similar spells.

"What are you going to do now?" Ellis asked.

Connor sighed. "We're going to walk the dog." He sounded tired and sad.

"What does that mean?" Ellis demanded.

"We are going to make a show of force and offer the enemy an opportunity to parlay," Connor clarified. The massive foot attached to Connor's rope pawed the ground, uprooting bushes and sending a head-sized boulder flying into the forest.

"What happens if they start shooting?" Ellis wondered. Far above her, onyx teeth flashed.

"We fight back," Connor stated.

"You can still stop this," Ellis pleaded.

"I cannot, any more than I could stop a river. I can merely divert its flow."

As Ellis opened her mouth to argue, her phone rang. The creature's head whipped toward her, and Ellis picked up the call before the noise could aggravate it further.

"*Ellis,*" Charlie shouted.

"Where are you?"

"I'm with Liza and Oscar out on Highway 2 north of La Cañada. Everything's blocked off. The LAPD sent a detachment to the Angeles National Forest, and I used my badge to sneak in. I'm going to try to make them see reason. Get them to call it off."

"Call what off?" Ellis' stomach dropped below the Earth's crust. "You can't stay there. You have to get out. Run as fast and far as you can."

The monster screamed again, and there was a long

silence on the phone. Before Ellis could speak, there was a loud whistle from the other side of the monster, and Connor walked forward, the magical leash gripped tight.

"What the hell was that?" Charlie asked. He might have heard the scream through the phone, but it was possible that it was audible on Highway 2. Ellis scrambled after her father, struggling to run and avoid rotting fish guts and talk on the phone at the same time. She wanted Charlie far away from the monster's glittering teeth.

"The drow are preparing a counter-attack," Ellis explained. "A dangerous one. You have to leave."

"I can't. Whatever the drow are planning, you have to stop them. The Army *will* retaliate. To be honest, they might strike first."

"*They'll regret it,*" Ellis shouted over the sound of tree trunks snapping beneath the shadow monster's feet.

There was a long pause. "We'll all regret it," Charlie agreed. "I gotta go. I'm going to try to stop this madness."

"Call if...I don't know. Call."

"I will."

"I love you," Ellis added, but Charlie had already hung up.

"What did he say?" Sebastian asked, scrambling behind her.

"Nothing good." Ellis trotted after the monster, away from the rising sun.

CHAPTER ELEVEN

The shadow mages and their monster moved more swiftly than Ellis would have expected from the elders. Part of it had to be adrenaline, but they all regularly sipped from small bottles tied to cords around their necks. Drow battle elixir—angry Gatorade fortified with energy-enhancing mushrooms and painkillers.

Later, Ellis would wonder how things had gone so wrong so quickly. The first sign of trouble came when an unmanned military drone flew over their party. The shadow monster did not *reach* up so much as *stand* up, its body unfurling until the jagged slash of its mouth was level with the sleek triangular drone.

As the drone banked away, the shadow monster opened its maw, teeth glistening. The monster's neck stretched out, and as the drone disappeared inside, the monster's mouth snapped shut. The noise was instantaneous, a crunching, sucking half-second. And then the drone was gone. Eaten? Impossible to say, although to Ellis, the dark fog that comprised the monster's body now looked blacker and denser. If that was what it did to metal and carbon, what would happen to a human body?

More importantly, how would the military react? Would they believe what they had seen? Barely stopping, the elders and Ellis and Sebastian continued their march across the forest, the shadow mages gripping their leashes.

Twenty minutes later, growling engines interrupted the silence of the forest. The military had taken the drone footage seriously enough to send planes. Fighter jets whistled in from an aircraft carrier stationed off the coast.

The monster ate the bombs they dropped. Ellis wouldn't have believed it if she hadn't seen it. The bombs plummeted from the planes, so small and far away at first that they looked like jimmies for ice cream. Then, the dark tendrils of the shadow monster's arms rose, dense and black, forking out like lightning to snatch the incoming ordnance.

Ellis could only wait, wondering if the bombs would blow sticky monster guts across the forest. If the bombs went off, there was no sign of it.

The drow kept moving. The monster was agitated. Had the bombs caused that? Worse, was it hungry? Connor's face became grayer and more strained as he poured shadow magic into the creature's bonds.

That strain reached a breaking point when they encountered the first military scouts. They had just transited a saddle between two hills, and Ellis had split from the group as they picked their way down a stretch of barren ground between thick stands of yellow-tipped Spanish broom. Ellis thought she heard something in the distance above and beyond the sound of the shadow beast crashing through the trees and shinnied up a nearby pine so she could see what was ahead.

Four Army Rangers had hunkered down behind a craggy outcrop. The monster was heading toward them on a diagonal, and one of the Rangers was setting up a long tube. Was it a grenade launcher?

She never found out because their leader issued a hushed command, and the shadow beast's head swiveled toward the Rangers. The soldiers raised their guns, but it was too late. As the jagged jaws descended on them, Ellis turned away. She couldn't bring herself to watch, but over the next few minutes, she heard four screams, then silence.

When her father shouted, she forced herself to follow the elders. Connor was winding between the trees, holding onto the monster's tether with both hands as the beast reared and pulled. When its body swung angrily toward Katya, the centrifugal motion spun Connor off his feet and yanked him a foot into the air. When he landed, he dug in, the shadow magic fetter stretching to the breaking point as the monster lunged toward the trees.

"Ellis!" Connor shouted, searching for her through the pines. Ellis raced toward him, swigging shadow magic potion. When she reached her father, she raised her hands to pour reinforcing shadow magic into his body.

"No," he countered, voice strained. "Go help Katya before we lose control."

Ellis thought that they already had.

The monster was currently walking on four black stalks with feet like wide suction cups. They made a dark, shifting arch, and Ellis caught sight of Katya on the other side. The elder speaker's skin was a bruised yellow, and she batted the snarling shadow monster with her staff.

Seeing her chance, Ellis dove between the monster's legs, ignoring her father's shout. It was astonishingly dark under there since the monster's foggy, shifting body absorbed the light. Also, the space between its torso and the ground was as cold as a walk-in freezer. A patch of blood beneath her had frozen into crimson crystals. Above her, the monster gnashed its teeth, a movement that produced a noise like a rusty industrial press.

Then she was on the other side. She used a fallen log as a springboard to leap to the elder speaker's side.

Katya was bent double with the effort of hanging onto the shadow magic leash, one hand slipping down the magical purple rope. Her other hand held her speaker's staff, which she plunged into the soil as an anchor.

"Let me help!" Ellis shouted as she reached the older woman.

Dense beads of liquid rolled down Katya's sallow skin and pooled in her wrinkles. The smooth metal of her speaker's staff was slick with sweat, and her ancient fingers were uncurling as the monster pulled the woman's arm out of its socket. Ellis poured shadow magic into Katya's body, reinforcing the speaker's waning power.

Katya turned wide, regretful eyes to Ellis as she lost her grip on the staff. Ellis reached for her hand, but Katya was yanked toward the monster like a palm frond in a hurricane. The monster's right arm snaked out and caught her in the middle of her torso, a blow that ended with a crunch. Then, the arm snaked around Katya's waist and carried her to the monster's mouth.

The elder speaker screamed for half a second. Then the monster's jaws clamped shut, and the cries were replaced with a horrible, muted grinding.

Freed from one of its restraints, the beast pawed the ground and surged west. As Ellis ran after it, she saw a faint purple thread streaming from one tentacle like a ribbon. It was the shadow magic leash; Katya had let go of it, but it hadn't been destroyed. If Ellis could catch it, she might be able to stop the monster before it wreaked more havoc.

The void sword shivered on her back. That was the other option. She could try to kill the monster.

A V-shaped formation of fighter jets crossed the sky. They weren't heading for the monster this time.

They were heading for the Homestead.

The magical tether flapped behind the monster, catching the sunlight, and Ellis sprinted toward it. They were in a dense part of the forest, so it took all her skill and energy to race after the monster. She wouldn't have been able to manage it, except that the monster was bulldozing the forest, a navigable swath of splintered trunks behind it.

Connor and the others were not holding the monster back so much as they were being towed behind it. *"Dad! Slow down!"* Ellis screamed. In the distance, Connor braced his legs against a tree. Her muscles burned, flooding with lactic acid as the monster screeched to a halt. The magical rope dangled between two pines, its glitter taunting Ellis.

Ellis sprinted, ears ringing as she lunged for the end of the rope. Just as her fingers grazed the magical surface, the monster reared onto its hind feet, and the rope whipped out of her grasp.

Ellis watched in horror as her father sailed through the air, no longer holding the purple tether. The ground shook beneath her as the monster stamped, but she barely felt it. She was running toward the spot where her father landed. "*Dad! Dad!*"

A black limb shot in front of her, blocking her path. The monster was turning on her. Ellis jumped back but slipped on a pile of dry pine needles. When she fell, the scabbard strapped to her back twisted her spine the wrong way, pinching a nerve.

The sword.

Ellis yanked it out from a sitting position. She had just adjusted her grip when the shadow monster's massive foot threw her into deep shade, blocking the sun as it plummeted toward her, on track to turn her two-dimensional. Ellis rolled, cutting it so close that the icy air coming off the monster's flesh gave her goosebumps. When the great paddle of a foot slammed into the ground, she swung the void blade into what served as its ankle.

To date, everything Ellis had cut with the void sword had parted easily beneath the blade. Metal, drywall, and flesh had all effortlessly fallen away. When the void blade contacted the monster's flesh, it was like a chainsaw hitting a titanium drill. The recoil nearly threw Ellis' shoulder out, and an icy whine screeched from the point of contact. Ellis grunted in pain and readjusted, forcing herself to drive the blade in farther.

The monster screamed in pain, which was good, Ellis decided, body straining to cut through the thick limb. Finally, the sword broke free, and the refrigerator-sized chunk of appendage she'd sliced off the monster exploded into mist. It burned where it touched her flesh, turning her skin white with frostbite. The monster slammed down on its freshly cut stump. There was no blood or exposed bone, just more black.

Where it touched the ground, the stump widened. The monster's leg reformed, and it once again stood on evenly-sized limbs.

It had regrown its leg like some demon starfish. In Ellis' opinion, that was incredibly rude. She scrambled to her feet, brandishing the sword even though the blade would not be effective. Several of the bulbous stalks on the monster's head swiveled toward her, and then it lumbered away.

Ellis considered going after it, but what was the point? The sword couldn't even put a dent in it, or not a lasting one.

A groan emerged from behind a nearby stand of trees, and Ellis located Connor. Sebastian was beside him, looking worried. As Ellis ran toward the men, an elder screamed behind her, and there was another crunch of bone and flesh.

Fury flashed through Ellis' chest. The elders had been stupid to summon the beast and even stupider to think they could control it. They had dragged her father into this mess, and now he was grievously wounded.

"What's wrong? Where does it hurt?" Ellis asked.

Her father's breathing was as shallow as an oily puddle. The trees had broken his fall, but they had also scratched him.

"My ribs," Connor reported.

"I think they're broken," Sebastian added.

Connor nodded faintly, a microscopic lowering of his chin.

Ellis uncorked the battle potion vial and held it to his lips. He drank as eagerly as he could, although his face paled as crushed foliage shifted beneath him, jostling his ribcage.

"You have to go after it," Connor urged.

"I'm not going anywhere."

He breathed again, and there was a wet, sucking noise. A bone shard had broken off his rib cage and gone into one of his lungs. He needed healing and fast. Closing her eyes, Ellis poured magic into her father's body, soothing the pain and knitting the worst breaks.

Sooner than she'd hoped, her reserves ran dry. The bottle of potion at her waist was empty, so Ellis reached for another in the satchel. Her father put his hand out. "You have to save your energy for what's ahead."

Her father was still in pain, but he would live. Reluctantly, Ellis put the bottle of shadow magic potion back in the bag. "Can you stand?" Ellis asked. He nodded. "Then come on. We'll go after it. Do you have any idea what it's going to do? Does it have plans? Or…instructions?"

"I don't think so. I think it's going to eat until it's full."

Ellis felt sick. "When is that?"

Connor just shook his head.

"I'm going to call Charlie. Stay with Dad," Ellis ordered Sebastian. He nodded.

Charlie's phone went straight to voicemail. Ellis numbly dialed again, which produced the same result. She wanted to throw the phone on the nearest rock and smash it like an otter smashed clams, but she carefully tucked it back into her pocket. She had confronted Charlie's death once before, and her mind now revolted, refusing to do it again.

There was a crash in the distance, then rifle fire. While her group did not see the first clash between the shadow monster and the military, they heard it. When the gunfire ceased, Ellis held her breath. Maybe her fears had been unfounded. Well, people had already died, so they weren't unfounded, but it was possible that the creature had been stopped.

Then the beast screamed. The sound was impossibly loud, ruffling the treetops as it washed up the mountains. It was *not* a cry of pain. It was the kind of thing you might hear from a triumphant warrior standing on a pile of enemy skulls.

Ellis' mind flashed back to her dream about the cave and the blurred words on the scroll. She felt the same way now—like she had a solution in her hands that she couldn't see. She climbed a tree in the hope of getting useful reconnaissance, but all she saw was the trail of destruction the shadow beast had left in the forest. It was heading straight for civilization.

If I want to go back for seconds, it won't be hard to track.

When she climbed down, Connor insisted he was ready to leave, but judging from the color on his face, he was still in shock. Ellis made him drink more battle magic potion and told him to rest for five more minutes. While the time ticked down, Ellis flipped between social media sites on her phone.

The shadow monster had made it to the city.

Most of the people online were reposting a TikTok

video from traffic at a dead stop on the 210. Even in an apocalypse, there was no escaping gridlock. The video was blurry but showed something black crawling onto an overpass and swallowing a VW microbus.

Ellis was sure it was the shadow monster. It played over and over on the screen as panicked people debated whether the governor had been right to impose a curfew in the comments. Apparently, all non-emergency personnel had been ordered to return to their homes immediately. Ellis wondered if the Calabasas mansion counted as her home.

As she tapped the LA Times app, an exclamation point popped up with a message that the phone had no service. She waited, hoping it was a temporary glitch, but no such luck. She was now in possession of a small and expensive paperweight. Maybe it was better not to know what havoc the creature was wreaking.

Cold seeped through her. She thought she was in shock until she realized the sensation was coming from the void sword. A paralyzing chill poured out of the black metal in an icy, enveloping fog. Once again, she thought about the statue and the scroll.

She crouched down beside her father. "I had a dream last night."

Connor frowned from more than pain. The drow didn't do prophecies or fortunetelling. "Not even the Mother Beneath knows what the future holds."

"I'm not sure this was a prophecy. I'm missing some critical piece of information. The *Encyclopedia Brittanica* isn't a prophecy about what happened during the war of 1812." Although he looked unconvinced, Ellis told him about the statue and the scroll. "I tried to read it, but the stupid mushrooms wouldn't give me enough light."

"What mushrooms?" Connor asked, now interested.

Ellis described the threadlike gold species she'd seen in her dream. Connor was quiet for a moment.

"Have you heard of them? Have you *seen* them?" Ellis asked. "Either of you?"

Sebastian shook his head. "We kept catalogs of drow species, but that's not my area. I don't recognize the description."

"I do." Connor cleared his throat with a wince. "In my errant youth, before I even went to Los Angeles and met your mother, a friend and I decided to sample every psychedelic mushroom we could find. The elders frown on their cultivation, but someone always has a cave full. The mushrooms you described sound like a species we looked for. Halo morels."

"That sounds about right," Ellis whispered, remembering the gold light around the statue's head. "Where did you find them?"

"We didn't." Connor shook his head. "Honestly, we did not look very hard."

"Where do halo morels grow?" Ellis asked.

"Out in Joshua Tree," Connor reported. "But that's a massive area. You can't just stumble around looking for mushrooms that are possibly extinct."

The fucking desert. Again. The thought of the shadeless expanses of dirt made her face feel hot, but Ellis sensed that that was where her path lay. "I have to try. It's important. I can feel it under my skin. Maybe it'll be like before when the ring helped me find the sword. Maybe the sword will know where to find the mushrooms."

"You'll have to get out of the forest first," Connor cautioned. "It might not be easy, given the increased military presence."

Ellis waved away his concerns. "That's what I was born to do."

"I would offer to go with you, but I am not sure I could make the journey." Ellis wasn't even sure he could make the journey back to the Homestead. However, his color was getting better, and he had managed to heal his lung where a bone shard had punctured it.

Ellis turned to Sebastian. "Take him back to the Homestead."

His eyes flashed in anger, and she grabbed his arm. "I can only leave if I know he's safe, and I have to go."

Sebastian wanted to argue, but in the end, he agreed. "I know it's selfish of me to want to see this through. I'll make sure he gets home safe."

It killed her to leave her dad, and she could tell he felt the same way, but there was no getting around it. As Connor hobbled into the forest, leaning on Sebastian, Ellis set her sights south.

The area was too large and densely populated for the government to cordon off the whole thing. Everything was in chaos, the roads so clogged with fleeing traffic that the military couldn't have evacuated all the houses bordering the Angeles National Forest if they had wanted to. Slipping through the patrols was easy.

It was harder to get transportation. Cell service was down, so she couldn't just call a Lyft. She decided that what she really needed was a motorcycle, which would be easier to get through the roadblocks and occasional crashes.

Acquiring one was easier said than done. Houses and garages were locked up tight, and valuable property had been taken off the streets. When she saw a motorcycle cop idling on a street corner, her heart soared. Ellis took a sip from her shadow magic potion and flung the man to a soft landing on a nearby lawn as she wrapped an invisibility spell around herself and the bike and zoomed away.

What should have taken three hours took nine. The cop's tank was nearly empty when she commandeered the bike, and it took threats of physical violence to convince the next gas station attendant she found to fill it up. There had been several multiple-car collisions along the 10, and Ellis frequently had to leave the highway to ride around them. As the sun dipped below the horizon, coating the landscape with beautiful but disorienting pink light, she pulled off the highway and wound up a road toward the national park.

Someone had set up a line of concrete pillars and a sign that said the park was closed. Ellis managed to walk the bike around without crushing many endangered cacti. After she was back on the road, she made good time.

She had hoped that when she got near the park, the sword would give her a sign. That it would be like the ring pulling her to some revelatory destination. Instead, it was an icy dead weight on her back. The supernatural cold was nice when it was light out, like magical air conditioning, but as her surroundings cooled off without the harsh light of the departing sun, Ellis shivered.

Lost and uncertain, Ellis stopped at the visitor's center

a few miles into the park. The lights were off and the doors were locked, and after a fruitless few minutes of trying to use a cactus spine as a lockpick, she dissolved the bolt and let herself in. She promised herself that she'd send the National Park Service a check to cover the damage when all this blew over.

When she was inside, Ellis turned on all the lights and wandered blankly between taxidermy dioramas and glass cases full of rocks. On a pedestal in the center of the room was a sign that said, *Open the panel to see the most dangerous animal in Joshua Tree National Park*. Ellis dutifully opened the panel and found a mirror. Cute. Clearly, the ranger who had designed this building had never seen a shadow monster.

I'll send a note with the check, telling them to update the display. Shuddering, she went over and looked at a large three-dimensional map covering one wall, reading the names of the rock formations and campsites.

When she saw a label on a rock formation just off the Barker Dam Trail, Ellis froze. The cold on her back was more intense.

Petroglyphs.

Ellis left the building at a run, the details of the map branded on her brain. She hit the gas hard when she reached the bike, pushing its performance as she rode the few miles to the trailhead. When she reached the parking lot, she debated hopping the motorcycle over the curb and steering it down the narrow single-track trail as far as it could go, but she decided she'd done enough damage to the national parks today. Anyway, she might need the bike to get back.

She trotted down the trail. Even this far from Los Angeles, the atmosphere was subdued. The animals knew that something in the world had tilted.

At first, Ellis was on flat ground, making good time through spiky stands of Joshua trees and yucca. Then smooth sandstone escarpments rocks rose around her path. This far from civilization, the sky was crystalline. Ellis tried to remember the last time she had seen so many stars. Soon, however, rock outcrops blocked her view. With the starlight and her half-drow vision, the landscape was easy to navigate.

When Ellis saw the petroglyphs, awe surged through her, rising like an errant wave on otherwise calm seas. The chiseled designs were simple but distinctive. There were several circles with forked lines branching out from their centers, a squiggle that looked like a snake, and a white shape that might have been a human figure. According to the pamphlet she had swiped from the visitor's center, the petroglyphs had been carved by the Cahuilla people, then painted over by Disney for a movie in the sixties.

When Ellis looked to one side of a lizard-like set of hatch marks on the wall, she froze. The spot attracted her, although all she could see was bare rock. Curious, she retrieved the bottle of potion from her backpack and took a sip. A bright purple mark appeared on the wall, the glow so intense that she had to shield her eyes.

The symbol was unmistakably drow, a tight whorled rune Ellis had seen on the walls in the Homestead's hallways.

Acting on instinct, Ellis withdrew the void sword from its scabbard. As she did, the quiet insect noises from the surrounding desert receded. Ellis raised the void sword and touched it to the center of the spiral, and the sandstone shifted.

As Ellis watched, an arch of solid rock turned to sand. Half the now-loose grains spilled onto the ground, and half flowed into the void sword, sucked in by some mystical force. Finally, the void sword shivered.

When Ellis looked at the rocks again, she saw a small tunnel. Dropping to her knees and replacing the sword in its scabbard, she crawled inside. The tunnel opened into a wider space a short distance in front of her, no more than six feet, and Ellis saw buttery yellow light in the chamber beyond.

The cave was smaller than she remembered. *Real estate is cheap in dreams.* The compact space made the profusion of halo morels covering the ceiling look dense and lush, like a thick crop of blonde hair. The statue in the center was as pale and solemn as it had been in her dreams. Ellis peered eagerly at its outstretched hand, but her fragile hopes sank when she saw that the palm was empty.

Ellis touched it, probing for invisibility spells. Her fingers brushed cool stone and nothing else.

Now that she was close to the statue, she saw that the walls behind it were covered with ideographs similar to the petroglyphs outside. The stick figures were the same, but there were subtle differences. First, many of the people in the drawings were blue or purple. Ellis guessed that the jewel-tone dyes had been produced from drow mushroom species.

Second, some of the figures were human, or Ellis

thought they were. Near the entrance tunnel, the glyphs showed rusty red figures chasing herds of deer with spears. In the corner, one of these red stick figures stood with a taller bright blue one. The ends of the stick figures' arms touched so that they looked like they were holding hands.

Just like humans, the drow had been here for a long time.

There was a faint rumble. The ground vibrated, and pebbles dropped from the ceiling. Then a golden mushroom dropped into the statue's hand, and the shaking stopped. Ellis froze. Although it had felt no different from the small earthquakes that regularly shook Los Angeles, Ellis doubted it was a coincidence.

She inspected the mushroom, remembering what her father had said about its psychedelic properties. She suspected she was supposed to consume it. *I doubt I'm supposed to put it in my hair.* She wished she had asked her father more questions about the mushroom's effects. What if it was poisonous? What if it interacted badly with the shadow magic potion?

She would have to take that risk.

Ellis downed the mushroom in a single bite, washing it down with water from a bottle in her pack. Then, she sat on the floor to wait.

It wasn't long before the light from the golden mushrooms on the ceiling began to curve and twist, bouncing off minute particles of dust that hung in the air after the earthquake. The light skipped across the statue, making the face of the hooded stone figure look alive.

The stone didn't move, but Ellis sensed a change in the

stern expression, a shift to something warmer and beatific. "Hello?"

The statue remained silent and smiling.

"I don't know where I'm supposed to go. I don't know what I'm doing."

The golden light got warm enough to give Ellis some relief from the chill of the void sword.

The statue didn't speak, but thoughts rose in Ellis' mind from a source inside the stone.

Your answers lie in another world.

"Very helpful. Does Delta fly there?"

The space between worlds is thin. You only need a door.

Ellis looked around the cavern, mystified. Getting unsteadily to her feet, she circled the chamber's perimeter, alert for another whorl. "Two hidden doors is overkill," she muttered to the statue.

The door does not exist yet.

Ellis decided that if she ever created a powerful magical artifact, she would write a nice instruction manual for it and put lots of copies near its arcane repository. Golden light crinkled in the statue's eyes, and bubbling laughter echoed in a far corner of Ellis' mind.

"This is really unfair. How am I supposed to find a door that doesn't exist?"

You are not meant to find it.

Annoyed, Ellis chucked a pebble at the statue. It bounced off the statue's face.

How did you find the Outpost?

A question mark echoed in her mind. "I *didn't* find the Outpost. I created it!"

Ah. The answer was obvious, like hair on her head. She

didn't have to go anywhere to find the door. It was with her right now. Ellis remembered what she'd thought the first time she'd seen the void sword. Question: what can it cut? Answer: anything.

She wasn't supposed to find a doorway.

She was supposed to make one.

Ellis unslung the sword from her back, wincing when she touched the hilt. Her body adjusted as she drew the black blade from its sheath. The sword made her feel cold and solid, and her breath became visible in front of her face.

The golden light was gone. The chamber looked dimmer, the twisting golden mushrooms like sickly snakes drooping from the vaulted rock ceiling. Ellis experimentally swished the blade. She had the feeling that she wasn't just moving molecules of oxygen around the blade. They were disappearing where the sharp edge touched. Or possibly she was slicing them in half. *Isn't that how nuclear fission works?*

She could worry about solving the energy crisis with a magic sword later. She hoped she would have time.

The statue had told her that the space between worlds was thin, but what did that mean? And where was it located? She hoped it wasn't somewhere weird, like in the lower atmosphere. That would make opening a magic door very tricky.

Ellis imagined the universe as a massive piece of paper, stretching out to infinity in all directions. If you laid a second flat universe on top of it, where would the space between worlds be? The answer was "everywhere."

She didn't need to go anywhere special. She could stay

right where she was. She stepped to the center of the room and raised the sword. Closing her eyes, she guided the blade with intention. She wasn't trying to cut air. She was looking for a gauzy break in the skin of the world.

The sword *snicked* through something. Ellis' breath caught, and the blade skipped. Moving carefully, she guided it back to the tiny divot she'd made in the ether, little more than a faint resistance in the air. She carefully widened the tear until she had a five-foot slit in the fabric of reality.

A dense column of purple fog massed before her. Waving her hand to clear it, she saw a second distinct reality, like she had cut a slit in the side of a circus tent and could watch the show in there. On the other side was the shadow world.

The sword had done its job. Ellis slid it back into its scabbard and slipped her hand into the tear between worlds. Dense shadow magic pressed against her skin. Ellis moved until her arm was inside, then added her right foot, testing for a solid surface. Her toes touched rock, so, moving cautiously, she slipped into the other world.

The fog surrounded her, filling her ears and nostrils. It was so difficult to see that, at first, Ellis wasn't sure she'd gone anywhere. She took two steps away from the slit, and when she looked back, she could hardly see it, covered as it was by purple mist. She wished she had a ball of string she could tie to the statue and unspool as she went.

A black shadow caught Ellis' eye, and for a moment, she feared it was the shadow monster. That was a horrible thought but not a crazy one. For all she knew, this was its home. Maybe she would find a nest full of shadow magic cubs. Worse, maybe the creature in Los Angeles was a baby, and she was about to meet its mother.

A section of the purple mist cleared, and Ellis realized that she wasn't looking at a shape. The shadow object was a wall constructed from head-high blocks of a dark stone identical to the smooth surface under her feet. Ellis decided to follow the wall.

After a moment, the purple fog closed back in, and the walk became disorienting. Without being able to see farther than her hand in front of her face, it was like being on a treadmill—difficult to tell if she was moving. The eerie motionlessness nauseated her, so when a doorway appeared, Ellis was relieved.

The stone door was etched with familiar drow patterns, but the doors were tall enough for a giraffe to walk through without ducking. Ellis wondered if she would be able to open them. Tentatively laying her palms on the panel, Ellis pushed. To her surprise, the hinges were well-maintained, and it slid open easily. Ellis only opened it enough to slip inside.

Her breath caught as she stared up. *Is there such a thing as reverse vertigo?* The ceiling was twice as tall as the door, a vaulted arch held up by smooth stone buttresses.

Had the drow once lived in places like this? The Homestead was comfortable, even beautiful in places, but it was nowhere near as massive as this. When Ellis' footsteps rang on the stone, the chamber swallowed the noise before they reached a surface to echo off.

At the far end of this antechamber was a vast staircase.

The first steps traversed the width of the room. Then the staircase narrowed until it became a person-wide slit at the top. This was definitely drow architecture. Someone had prepared to defend themselves against invisible intruders.

Ellis considered turning invisible, but she had not encountered anyone yet, so it seemed like a waste of potion. She went to the stairs.

The climb knocked the breath out of her. How far had she walked, and how many feet had she ascended? There was visual trickery going on with the scale. She stopped when she reached the top and gulped water from her backpack. She wanted to splash some on her face, but there was no telling when she'd be able to resupply. Maybe water didn't exist in this realm.

The room at the top of the stairs was built on a smaller scale, with rows of long stone benches facing a large dais. It supported a massive etched throne with lacy layers carved from the stone of the platform. The throne wasn't the only thing on the dais. Peeking out from behind its base was the edge of a cot covered in a crystal silk blanket.

The bedding looked so ordinary that it failed to register as a threat, but as Ellis circled the throne, the blanket moved, and a dark blue man sat bolt upright, screaming when he saw her. Ellis yelped in surprise, scrambling to unsheathe her void sword.

The drow she had startled peered down the length of the blade. He looked more surprised by her presence than by the sword.

"Hello," Ellis greeted, voice soft.

The man nodded.

"My name is Ellis." She kept the sword up but took a

half-step back. It was difficult to tell if the drow understood her. "Ellis," she repeated, putting her hand on her chest.

The man touched his chest. He opened his mouth, then coughed. When he spoke, his voice wavered, his mouth shaping his words uncertainly. "Hello, Ell-is."

"You understand me?"

He opened his mouth, then froze. When he finally spoke, his voice was reedy. "I...have not spoken to another person...in a very long time. You are human?"

"Yes." It was true, if incomplete.

"But...you are also...a drow..." He took that in stride, which put her at ease.

She smiled. "That's right. Drow dad, human mom. Do you live here?" She glanced at the cot. He looked as old as Ellis' father but was thinner, his deep blue skin stretched across angular bones. His coverlet of worn crystal silk looked ordinary in the hall, a rectangle of reality in an unreal place.

"I am here," he replied carefully. That wasn't the same thing.

"Have you been here for a long time?"

He nodded.

Ellis flipped through a wide range of questions. *Wanna show me around? What do you know about magic swords? Come here often?* "What's your name?"

The drow paused like he was struggling to remember. Ellis guessed that he'd been alone for a long time.

"Falco." He smiled brightly, like an eager student with his hand up.

"Hello, Falco." Without letting go of the sword, she

shrugged the backpack off her shoulder, undid the back pocket, and retrieved a wrapped tunnel bar from inside. She held it out. "You look hungry. Here."

The bar was gone before she finished talking. Falco unwrapped it and ate it in small but frantic bites.

"I...I haven't had food in a..." His voice trailed off, expression suddenly remote.

"What do you eat?" Ellis asked curiously. There must be food here since he was still alive, but the atmosphere didn't scream "agricultural bounty."

"I make food from the mist," He waved in the direction of the hallway and door.

"You *make* it?" Ellis had never heard of such a thing.

"It is difficult." He reached into his pocket. Ellis tensed, following the movement with the sword, and Falco withdrew several dense lumps of an ashy purple substance. It looked like Play-Doh and seemed as appetizing. Was that how he'd survived?

Ellis pulled off a tiny piece and tasted it. It wasn't bad, a flavorless substance with a slight chalky aftertaste. When she swallowed, however, shadow magic tingled on her tongue. Somehow, Falco converted the shadow magic energy into food.

"Needs ketchup." Ellis grinned.

Falco frowned, not knowing what that was. "I have a warning."

Ellis tensed and looked down the staircase into the great hall. Behind the throne, a door led deeper into the fortress, or whatever this place was. They didn't appear to be under attack from either direction. Falco corrected, "I have a...story."

Which is it, buddy? A story or a warning? Most fairytales were both.

"Tell me your story." Ellis tried to look encouraging. Taking a leap of faith, she lowered the sword.

Falco looked at the shadow magic crumble in his hand, struggling to remember why he was holding it. He plucked off a small chunk and ate it without relish, then offered what was left to Ellis.

"I don't want to fill up on edible shadow magic Play-Doh before dinner," Ellis refused. Looking relieved, he returned the purple lump to his pocket.

Formalities out of the way, Falco sank to the dais, leaning against the back of the throne. Ellis sat down cross-legged opposite him. He was silent for a moment, assembling his thoughts. When he spoke, his voice was stronger and more fluid. Confident, as if he'd been practicing this for a long time.

"I am the last of my people," Falco began, "and I have lived for a long time."

Ellis nodded encouragingly, not wanting to interrupt his flow.

"Once upon a time, below the surface of the world, there was a homestead. A drow community, much like any other. The rangers harvested the food and animals above, and the miners harvested the rock and metal below.

"Near the Homestead's entrance, there was a human village. Sometimes, the humans would bring the drow goods to trade, and the two peoples lived together in peace. Sometimes, when a human was ill, they would go into the caves near their village and cry out for help. When the drow heard them, they would bring potions and sometimes healing magic. It was that way for a long time.

"One day, the village headman's young daughter got ill. He brought her to the caves and called out for help. The drow appeared, as they usually did, and their healers brought potions and wisdom. However, the girl's illness was too severe, and she died.

"The headman's grief was terrible, and he went mad. He became convinced that the drow healers had sickened his daughter with their magic and killed her with their potions. The drow thought that his grief would fade in time, and perhaps it would have.

"It never did because, blinded by grief, the headman assembled the greatest warriors of his village to raid the drow's caverns. Every drow man, woman, and child was slaughtered in a berserker rage, for there were witches among the humans who could protect them from the drow's shadow magic. Only one drow escaped."

He paused. Ellis could guess who the lone escapee was.

"How did you escape the warriors?" Ellis asked.

"I had a human lover. It was summer, and we were together in the forest, hunting, bathing in the river, and harvesting wild berries. When she returned to her village, the headman accused her of collaborating with the enemy and had her killed." Falco's voice was remote, as if he were reporting something he'd seen in a dream when he was a child.

Ellis wondered again how long he'd been here. "I'm so sorry."

"I returned to the tunnels and caves, but the Homestead was gone. For a time, I drank no water and ate no food. I went into the deepest reaches of the tunnels and lay in the darkness, willing myself to die, but I could not. My mind was too awake with psychic pain.

"The Mother Beneath had not welcomed my people's spirits to her domain, and they surrounded me, yanking me back into the world each time I neared death. With the last of my strength, I begged the Mother Beneath to let me rejoin my people and to welcome us all into the caverns below the world.

"I had grown very weak, and when a greater darkness covered my eyes, the Mother Beneath appeared to me, shrouded in layers of shadow. She asked me to live. I told her that it was too late, and without food, I would not have the strength to return to the tunnels. Her voice rang in my head like a dark bell, and she taught me how to draw sustenance from the shadows."

"The Play-Doh," Ellis whispered.

He cocked his head at the new word.

"The Mother whispered in my ears for days, coaxing me to eat. At her command, a spring welled up beside me, and I drank deep from its dark water. When my strength returned, I understood what I had to do."

"You summoned the shadow beast."

"No, I *created* the shadow beast. That was why the Mother Beneath refused to welcome my people's spirits. I needed them for my dark arts."

"You created the shadow beast from *drow spirits*?"

"Yes. The beast is a manifestation in the world of their pain and rage. Carrying me to the surface on its back was its last act of kindness. Untethered from the physical world, my people's spirits became cruel. Existing in the physical world without living was excruciating. They yearned to return to flesh and bone, and it drove them to blind consumption.

"As the beast reached the mouth of the cave and clawed its way across the moonlit forest toward the human village, I knew I had made a terrible mistake, and I was now no different from my enemies, but I was too weak to correct it. When the monster returned, claws dripping with blood, satiated and sluggish, I set to work restraining it. I locked it behind three powerful shadow spells."

"And you didn't leave an instruction manual," Ellis muttered.

"No. I intended the knowledge to die with me, but I had thwarted the Mother Beneath's plans for revenge, so after I restrained the beast, she banished me here."

"Where *are* we?"

Falco shrugged. "I don't know. It's the Mother's realm. An endless void of shadows, raw rock, and magic."

"Maybe it's her summer home," Ellis mused. Falco didn't laugh. He probably didn't remember what summer was. She cleared her throat. "So, who built this place?" She swept her hand across the throne room.

"I did."

Ellis gaped. "What? With who?"

"Who?" He looked confused. "I built it myself. With shadow magic. From the rock."

"All of it?" Ellis remembered the scale of the front door.

"I made lots of mistakes at first. After many failed attempts, I learned a great deal about construction. There was nothing else to do, so I built myself a castle. For a time, I thought of myself as the king. The ruler of an empty land.

I thought this place would be my life's great work." He tapped the throne with one long finger. "I thought when I completed it that I would die, but death never came. I persist. I grew bored with architecture." Falco looked like he'd grown bored with everything.

"The Mother Beneath just left you here?"

He shrugged. "She might have forgotten about me. She has rages. Did she send you, too?"

What a question that was. Was it possible she was being punished for working with the humans? Ellis hoped not. If the deity had called her to this task, no one had forwarded Ellis the message. "I-I don't think so. I don't know. I came in here on my own. With this." She raised the sword to waist height.

"Who gave you the sword?"

"I...found it." It wasn't a lie.

"Are you here to free me from this realm?"

"Not specifically. I'm trying to stop the shadow monster. My Homestead released the three spells that kept it prisoner, and it's about to kill a lot of people."

"Humans? Your kin?"

"My friends. Also my kin, I guess." Percy was nothing if not a crazy uncle. And Charlie? Charlie's survival and well-being were non-negotiable. Also, Claire was out there somewhere. "Is that surprising? My background?"

Falco shook his head. "Such cases are known. Rare, but known."

Very interesting. She would ask about it after she defeated the regenerating shadow monster made of angry drow souls. "Please. How do I stop the beast?"

"It would be better to stop the drow from summoning it."

"I agree, but it's too late for that. Is there something we can do?"

Ellis thought he was staring at the sword, but then she realized he was looking at the ring on her finger. Specifically at the pearl. *It's a promise ring. A promise to slice stuff up with a sword.*

"Do you recognize this?" she asked, holding up her hand.

"Yes. There is a similar pearl inside the monster. Larger than that one, perhaps the size of a fist. The monster's heart. A dense, calcified organ pulsing with shadow magic and spirits. Cut it out."

"Is that all?" Ellis asked drily.

Falco frowned, not picking up on the sarcasm. "It will not be an easy task. The beast is powerful."

Ellis sighed. "There's not some, say, magic arrow I can shoot it with from a distance?"

"No archer I know could make that shot. No, you must use the sword." He looked at it curiously.

Ellis sighed. She had suggested using an arrow as a joke, but this would come down to the same thing it always did: getting in something's face and punching. *But with a sword.*

"By destroying the beast, you will free my people's spirits," Falco continued.

Now she was responsible for human lives *and* drow souls. After standing up, Ellis nodded. "I'm very sorry for what happened to you. I'll do what I can. Will you come with me? Your knowledge could prove useful."

He looked eager. He had not thought that he would ever leave this place. "If I can. How did you get here?"

Ellis wondered if she could find the spot where she'd entered the shadow realm. It was outside in the mist. She and Falco could wander for hours without finding it, and for all she knew, it had closed. She hoped the process she'd used to get here would work in reverse.

"Stand back, and I'll show you." Falco crept dutifully away, and Ellis stepped into the open space behind the throne, closed her eyes, and raised the sword.

This time, it was easier. Within seconds, the tip of the blade caught on the skin of reality, and the resulting slit revealed a sand-colored world. This was promising, but Ellis approached it cautiously. What if this new door dropped them back on Earth a hundred feet in the air above spiky rocks? What if it took them to another world that was neither Earth nor the shadow realm? Falco circled the slash, frowning at the bright edges where the throne room became another world.

Ellis peered inside, relieved when she saw a hooded statue in the room beyond. Mist poured through the gap into the desiccated California cave. The sword apparently had its own metaphysical GPS.

"Let's go." Ellis stepped through, then pulled Falco through. He emerged into the cave, frozen in awe at the sight of the vibrant ideographs. Falco hadn't seen anything new in a very long time. No surprise that he was overwhelmed.

When he reached for a halo morel, Ellis grabbed his hand. "We'll find you some real food, I promise, but there's a lot to do. I can't afford to have the ancient dark elf I just dragged out of a pocket shadow realm tripping balls."

Falco looked confused.

"Those mushrooms will make you see weird stuff." A motorcycle trip through modern Los Angeles would also make him see weird stuff, but Ellis didn't mention that.

She glanced at the hooded statue before they crawled out of the cave. The golden light of the halo morels had returned, and it seemed to be smiling.

CHAPTER TWELVE

Ellis gave Falco the helmet for the ride to Los Angeles. In the new day's sunlight, he seemed even frailer than he had looked in the ancient cave. She wished she had a shape-changing medallion to give him. If they got into trouble, they would have to turn invisible and slip away.

She could barely trust him to hold onto her waist. Falco was dazed, head swiveling in all directions as they cut through the desert and back into the city. There was a police barrier where the 10 turned into the 101, and Ellis barely kept her invisibility spell active as she guided the bike between two barriers.

Falco's fingers gripped her waist so tightly that she winced. As she was about to ride away, she paused and steered the bike onto the shoulder fifty feet from the barricade. Running around blindly would only get her so far.

Flicking on a cloaker, she handed it to Falco and told him to stay put.

"Where are you going?"

"To get directions." Ellis moved toward the detachment.

The cops had put up temporary barriers and manned them, but by this point, no one was trying to get into the city, so they were holed up on the side of the road behind a curved wall of sandbags. Only two cops were stationed here. The county's police forces were spread thin. The officers, a woman and a man, looked simultaneously bored and terrified. That was a dangerous combination, and Ellis unsheathed the void sword as she crept toward the sandbag wall, just in case.

"At least we're out of it," the woman was saying. "We've got the whole US Army between us and…whatever that thing is."

"You believe the videos?"

"Little purple men? Monsters? Shit, I don't believe anything anymore."

In the distance, Ellis heard artillery fire.

"I haven't heard that sound since Iraq," the man remarked. "I hoped I'd never hear it again, especially on US soil."

"Where do you think the mortars are landing?"

"Last I heard, that thing was headed north, tearing up the 101."

"Maybe it'll take out Bakersfield instead of us."

"Hey, there's a silver lining to everything."

The cops chuckled, but the tension under the gallows humor was unmistakable.

North it is. She walked back to the bike.

Falco was standing glumly, looking over the railing at the city. "This is a large village."

"Yeah, it is."

Falco nodded. "Do you have a plan?"

"I don't want to go after the beast alone," Ellis stated. That wasn't true. She didn't want to put anyone else at risk, but it wouldn't be smart to go this one alone with so many lives at stake. And since the city was crawling with military and law enforcement, there was a chance that she'd run into trouble before she got to the monster. *I swear, Officer, I'm just holding this magic sword for a friend.*

"I want to find Charlie," Ellis announced, making the decision as she said it. "He's a friend of mine, a cop. That's a ranger who is responsible for protecting the city. Sort of. Some of them are thieves and assholes…" Her voice trailed off. Now was not the time for a lecture about police corruption. "Charlie can help get us to the monster." *And I'll take it from there.*

"Where is this friend?" Falco asked. "It must be difficult to find people in a village this size."

"He was out near the forest. I'd bet a million bucks he followed the monster."

"What is a buck?" Falco asked.

Ellis shrugged. Now was also not the time for a lecture on the modern US monetary system. "It's, like, half a tunnel bar." She revved the engine before Falco could ask more questions.

The cops had been right about having the military between them and the monster. The roads soon became clogged with gray-green trucks, and half the people on the streets wore body armor. Sirens and roadblocks were ever-present, and it became clear that Ellis would never be able to go north on the highways, even if she could stay invisible the whole time.

She took an offramp when she hit downtown. They would have to take their chances in the city.

They hadn't worried about speed limits out in the desert since the cops had more important things to do than enforce traffic laws, but now that they were in Los Angeles, the roads were choked with abandoned cars. Most of the people they encountered were military or law enforcement, hauling around the biggest guns they'd been able to check out of their armories. The drone of helicopters filled the air. She would never find Charlie by driving around.

She and Falco got off the bike and stalked the streets until they found two cops loitering in the shade of a grassy median below where Hollywood ascended into the hills. Ellis explained her plan to Falco, who seemed familiar with the principles of strategy and tactics.

"Do you know about guns?" she asked suddenly. He told her he didn't, which worried her. Fortunately, or unfortunately, depending on how her plan unfolded, the cops were armed with rifles and handguns, which gave Ellis plenty of show-and-tell fodder.

How do you explain a gun to an elf who's thousands of years old and has been alone most of that time? She did her best. It was like a bow and arrow, only louder. "Just stay away from the end with the hole," she finally ordered, hoping it would be enough.

The cops' attention was focused on the hillside, where flashes of light accompanied the booms of artillery fire. The explosions were very loud, and both cops were wearing ear protection, which made them easier to sneak up on. Descending on them invisibly, Ellis and Falco sprang. He grabbed the smaller cop as she held the larger one at swordpoint.

"*No one move, and it'll all be okay,*" Ellis shouted.

Her hostage's eyes were fixed on his partner. More specifically, on Falco. They widened as he took in the blue skin and pointed ears.

"You're one of the aliens."

"We're not aliens!" Ellis huffed. "We're magical cave elves."

"*We?* Shit, you're one of them." The cop's bushy eyebrows quivered above wide eyes. "They're shapeshifters, Gary."

"We're not shapeshifters!" Not without the crystal-charged medallions, but this wasn't the right time to school these men on the finer points of shadow magic. "We're just people."

"People who sicced a big-ass monster on us," the cop named Gary rebutted.

"If someone sent a battalion of heavily armed Rangers to your home, what would you do? My people are afraid."

"Well, so are we," the tall cop shot back.

"I'm on your side, sort of. I'm going to try to stop the shadow monster. You can choose to believe me or not, but will you help me? I need to find a friend of mine. A cop. Charlie Morrissey."

The cop's eyes widened, and Ellis realized he looked familiar. "You're one of Ron Jackson's goons." The man scowled at that characterization, which told Ellis she was right. What was his name again? She glanced at his badge, which said Fred Humphrey. "Fred." The name rang a bell, although not a loud one.

"I was never on board with Jackson's shenanigans. He threatened my kid." Humphrey took in Ellis' black boots and waves of black hair, held back by a thin elastic. Realization flooded his eyes. "Holy shit. You're Charlie Morrissey's pet vigilante!"

Gary eyed Ellis suspiciously. He looked like he wanted to poke Ellis to see if she was real, and he might have done it if Ellis hadn't been holding a sword. He just shook his head in disgust. "At this rate, next year, the mounted unit is gonna be riding unicorns."

Ellis smiled grimly, wiggling the sword to remind the cops she was in charge. "I'm glad my fame has preceded me, but I need you to focus, Gary! I have to find Charlie."

"Or what?"

"Or you're going to learn how well your body armor works against a magic sword," Ellis growled. The blade vibrated enthusiastically, emitting a low hum that drained the blood from the cops' faces.

Gary didn't want to find out, so he raised his radio. "Central, hey. Yeah, haven't seen any movement. Listen, I need a location on Officer Charlie Morrissey. Do you have a badge number?" he asked Ellis.

"No."

"Charlie Morrissey in Homicide," the cop offered.

The radio crackled. "Just a sec." The silence was excruciating, and as it drew out, Ellis wondered if the LAPD's computers were still working. Finally, the dispatcher came back on. "He volunteered for the team going after the monster." She relayed the information like it was a fatal diagnosis.

"You know where he is now?" Gary asked.

Another pause, then, "No. The military isn't playing nice with us. Fucking ground-pounders. They think we'll steal their thunder. Is there anything else? I gotta go."

Gary said goodbye and looked fearfully at Ellis. "I'm sorry. That's all there is."

Ellis tapped her foot impatiently as an artillery blast rattled the hillside. "Where is the monster?"

The tall cop shrugged. Gary sneered. "Follow the screaming," His eyes darted to the hills. Ellis made the two men lie face-down on the grass and told them to count to a hundred before getting up. She never found out if they'd obeyed her order since in seconds, she and Falco were winding up the road into the hills.

The air was thick with smoke, and several canyons over, the hills' crest glowed orange, presumably where the artillery had ignited the brush. Ellis was used to using muffling spells to keep conversations in. Now she had to reverse the magic, creating a bubble around herself and Falco to keep the punishing artillery booms from imploding their eardrums.

The local birds had intelligently vacated the sky. All that was left above were drones, which were clustered one valley over. Ellis pointed. "That way." They picked their way through the underbrush on the hill, dissolving privacy fences with shadow magic when the brush-choked slopes gave way to hillside homes.

Gary's sarcastic comment about following the screaming proved prescient. They heard a high, terrified wail. Even from a distance, the keening pierced the muffling spell.

"It's coming from the Hollywood Bowl." Ellis took off running, abandoning the bike.

The Bowl was a massive open-air amphitheater in the Hollywood Hills, which had opened in the early twenties with a local high school's production of *Twelfth Night*. The venue usually had a music festival atmosphere, attracting people who wanted to drink BYOB wine with their picnics and listen to big musical acts. Ellis had been there once to see the LA Philharmonic play a live score during a screening of Indiana Jones. Now, the Bowl's excellent acoustics amplified terrified screaming.

Why hadn't the area been evacuated? Traffic had always been a problem at the venue, and now, every road leading into the hills was a parking lot. Later, Ellis learned that instead of evacuating the amphitheater the day before, the military had sent a large detachment to protect it, reasoning that it was safer to shelter everyone in place. That meant the military had served the monster a captive audience in a bowl. *All the monster needs is a spoon.*

Whatever control the military had over the situation had been lost some time ago. As Ellis ran up the steep asphalt road that led to the venue, she had to fight a fleeing crowd streaming around abandoned parked cars. She could not fight these people and maintain invisibility, so it was time to play "The Floor is Lava." Or in this case, "The Floor is Screaming Tourists."

Ellis pulled Falco on top of the nearest car. From her new vantage point, she surveyed the terrain, looking for police detachments. Just when she was about to give up, she saw the SWAT van, which was really an armored bus. It was parked in a utility lot below the Bowl's entrance, surrounded by a group of well-armed cops.

Ellis saw a familiar head of short brown hair, and just before Charlie put his helmet on, she screamed his name. With the muffling spell surrounding her, he didn't hear her. The police looked like they were about to move out, so she had to work fast.

Shouting for Falco to follow, Ellis leapt six feet to the top of a maroon minivan, cracking its sunroof as she landed. She yanked her foot away as the glass shattered inward. Ellis winced and checked the back seat, but the van was empty.

Falco landed more lightly, and they jumped to the next car and the next like frogs on lily pads. When she was ten feet from the SWAT van, she jumped with all her strength. It was a stretch, but she made it, landing on the roof with a loud metallic clang. A police officer below looked up. It was Liza, geared up for battle. Ellis also recognized Oscar Velasquez.

After making sure Falco's cloaker was on, she told him to stay on the bus. She leapt onto the asphalt and dismissed her invisibility spell.

"Charlie!" she shouted. The man she yelled to was wearing a helmet with a full face mask. She hoped she hadn't been mistaken about his identity. This time, he heard her, and the second he enfolded her in a hug, she knew it was him. She would know those shoulders anywhere. She heard him suck in a breath as his hand touched the icy scabbard across her back.

When she pulled away, she realized there were six guns pointed at her: two automatic rifles and four handguns.

She had not taken her own advice about staying away from the ends with the holes. She didn't recognize the officers behind them. The silver lining was that Liza and Oscar hadn't drawn their weapons. Charlie raised his hands slowly, then removed his helmet. Ellis didn't move.

"Guys, it's okay," Charlie called.

"*Who the fuck is that?*" an officer with an automatic rifle shouted.

"This is Ellis," Charlie replied carefully.

"It's okay, everyone," Liza added.

"Ellis is one of us," Oscar agreed.

"*What the fuck do you mean? What unit is she with?*" the smallest of the officers shouted. She sounded afraid, and the tip of her handgun quivered with nerves.

"She's not a cop," Charlie told them.

"But she's on our side," Liza added, sounding like she was trying to convince herself it was true.

"Take off the weapon and put it on the ground," the rifle cop shouted.

The void sword thrummed on Ellis' back, the vibrations intense. "I can't."

"What the fuck do you mean, you can't?"

"I need it to stop the shadow beast," Ellis continued.

Liza glanced at the sword. "That beast eats L15 high explosives, and that's not a metaphor. I saw it chew up one of the shells. You can't just walk up and fucking stab it."

"I'm not going to."

"Okay, then." Liza sounded relieved.

"I'm going to cut its heart out," Ellis clarified.

Liza did not look comforted. "You're going to lead Charlie into certain death. That's what you're going to do."

"I can do this, really. I...learned a little more about the creature from a friend. Falco? Come on down here."

After a moment, Falco appeared on top of the bus. The officers murmured in surprise, and about half the guns pointed at Ellis turned on Falco as he leapt lightly down on the asphalt.

He pointed at the nearest gun. "Ellis told me to stay away from the end with the holes."

"Good advice," Liza agreed drily.

Oscar snorted. "Fuck. You're one of the...the drow."

Charlie nodded.

"Charlie has been hammering us on vocabulary," Liza explained. "He says we can't call 'em purples or MECs or aliens."

"For Pete's sake, we're not aliens!" Ellis exclaimed. "Drow is good. You can also call us dark elves."

The cops looked unenthusiastic. Ellis groaned. "Look, you can call me whatever you want if you get me close enough to stab the shadow monster." The cops shuffled around. Two lowered their guns, but no one responded. Ugh. It was time for some razzle-dazzle.

"Look, Falco is... Falco was there when the monster was created. He knows how to stop it. I know how to stop it too. I'm going to use *this*." Ellis unsheathed the sword. In the sunlight, the blade looked impossibly black, like an abyss in a dim cave. A wave of cold air pulsed out of it, although the drops of condensation that produced were immediately sucked back into the blade. The cops looked impressed but also afraid. Liza put her hand on her gun.

There was another scream from the direction of the Bowl. The cops swiveled toward the noise.

"Please," Ellis begged. "Help me."

The rest of the guns went down.

"What do you need?" Liza asked.

"I need to get close to its chest."

"Oh, is that all?" Oscar gave a dark chuckle.

"Yes. That's all."

There was a brief whispered conference. Then Charlie said, "If anyone has a better idea, I'm open to it."

No one spoke.

"All right. Well, in that case, we'll follow Ellis' plan. *Let's go!*"

"We'll never get in the main doors," Liza gestured toward where the crowd of people was pouring out.

"We'll go in over the top. Via the hillside." When Charlie looked at Ellis, there was a devilish glint in his eye. "By the way, I stopped by the evidence lockup when I went back to the station. I thought I might run into you, and I picked up a little gift."

He unclipped a bulky but familiar item from his waist belt and handed it to her.

"My grappling gun!" Ellis squealed, then clamped a hand over her mouth. You weren't supposed to squeal when you were asking a bunch of burly cops to trust your swordsmanship. She beamed at Charlie as she inspected the gun, checking the mechanisms for rust or tampering. It looked perfectly maintained. It was her spare, which she'd left at her condo after the fire. Apparently, the police had seized it as evidence.

"Thank you." Ellis turned a full-wattage smile on Charlie, who looked pleased with himself. The screaming and chaos from the Hollywood Bowl put a damper on their good cheer, and they got back to work. Ellis fell into step behind Charlie as he led the LAPD detachment around the amphitheater's perimeter wall.

Ellis grinned as she used the grappling gun to top the wall, then lowered a fire ladder to bring the cops up behind her. Once they were all on the wall, Ellis crouched and assessed the scene, trusting her cloaker to keep her hidden. A teeming mass of people had clustered at the low point of the auditorium, pushing and shoving to reach any exit. Someone screamed, and Ellis saw the monster in the cheap seats.

It was bigger than it had been in the forest. More solid, too. Its foggy black skin had condensed into shifting scales that rippled as it moved toward a young man who was trying to exit the auditorium by scaling one of the plaster walls. All of its eye stalks were focused on him as its many legs poured across the rows of aluminum benches.

"*No!*" Ellis shouted and leapt down the concrete stairs two at a time. It was too late. Before Ellis got near the monster, it sprang forward and batted the man into the air with an arm the diameter of a redwood tree. Rearing with its toothy maw wide, it swallowed the body with a single sickening crunch like it was a tossed popcorn kernel.

Charlie ran up behind her. His knuckles were white on his rifle, and his voice wavered when he spoke. "What do we do?"

The benches rattled as the monster's front feet slammed down. It let out a low growl, and its eyestalks turned in the direction of the escaping crowd. There had to be a hundred people down there.

"We have to protect the exit," Ellis stated.

The monster was moving slowly, like a well-fed but bored lion. Its massive limbs thumped downward one by one. Aluminum benches buckled beneath its weight with squeals, setting Ellis' teeth on edge as she bounded down to put herself between the monster and the crowd. The void sword thrummed in her fist as she raised it, angling it across her body with both hands.

The monster skidded to a stop when it saw her and let out a low whine.

"*Try me!*" Ellis shouted.

A shot rang out. The monster's head jerked faintly, and its eyestalks turned to its right. Charlie had taken up a firing position on the stairs, and as the shadow beast turned, he put a bullet into the monster's maw. One of its massive teeth split in half and fell onto the concrete.

The monster screamed in pain and lunged toward him.

Ellis acted out of blind panic, sprinting up the stairs toward the impossibly long forearm hurtling at Charlie. He fired three more shots, but the incoming limb absorbed them. When he decided to run, it was too late.

A blast of cold air raised goosebumps on Ellis' skin as she raised the sword and sliced through the shadow monster's arm. Cutting into the monster's flesh was a jarring agony, but Ellis managed it. After she cut through the final few inches, Charlie was blasted with frozen shadow dust instead of solid mist. The monster screamed in pain and scrambled toward the top levels of the amphitheater. Ellis advanced on it, sword in hand. The cops arrayed below the wall fired at the retreating beast, but it seemed to ignore their bullets.

She looked for an opening inside its guard, but as she

moved toward the monster, it backed away from the sword with a cry of pain. The plaster crumbled as it reached the top of the wall. To Ellis' surprise, it crawled over the barrier.

She hadn't expected it to retreat, but even a creature that could regrow its limbs might not enjoy the process. It was good to know that she could scare it.

Ellis ran to Charlie, who was brushing acrid-smelling black dust off his face.

"Are you okay?" she asked.

He nodded, slowly regaining his bearings. "I think so."

There was a crash on the other side of the wall as something heavy moved through the urban forest. "I have to go after it," Ellis told him.

Charlie grabbed his gun with a wince and straightened. "Yeah. We'll regroup."

"There's no time, and there's no point in you coming."

"What?"

"You saw how that thing reacted to bullets. It might even *like* them. It's afraid of the sword."

"You should still have backup."

"I will go with her." Falco had joined them on the steps, holding a jagged object—the monster's shattered tooth. The black thing was sharp, and looking at it made Ellis uneasy. She couldn't spend any more time arguing. The monster's retreat was already inaudible beneath the screaming and the artillery fire.

"Don't worry about me." As Ellis sprinted toward the top of the Bowl, she replaced the void sword in its scabbard and grabbed the grappling gun. Ten feet from the wall, she pulled the trigger. When the hook caught, she ordered Falco to grab her waist and retracted the wire. They ran up the wall and sailed over the top, and Ellis twitched the hook off with a flick of her wrist. The momentum carried them over in a wide arc. She landed between two trampled elm trees, knees bending, and rolled. It was hard on her joints, but she made it back to her feet without injury.

Falco, a few feet behind her, fared even better, and he ran past her with a light stride. Whatever else he had done in the shadow realm, he had stayed in shape. Ellis scrambled after him.

The monster's path of destruction through the stretch of scrub just below the Hollywood Bowl was easy to follow, although a few times, Ellis stumbled as her boot plunged through a pile of broken branches. They crossed a road and ran past a trampled shed that sat at the low point between two houses. When they reached one of the Hollywood Hills' winding roads, Ellis pulled Falco down the slope to the left. "Path of least resistance," she wheezed between deep breaths.

Unfortunately, the road twisted, and by the time Ellis realized she'd chosen wrong, it was too late to go back. She had always hated this part of town for exactly this reason. "Just keep going downhill. We'll find that thing eventually." Hopefully not because of screaming, but you never knew.

When they reached the flats, Ellis was forced to admit they had lost their quarry. She staggered to a stop in the middle of Highland Avenue, listening for crashes or screams in the distance. Instead, she heard a coo. There was a pinprick of pain at her wrist, and Ellis looked down to see an odd-eyed pigeon pecking her hand.

"Wormy?" Ellis asked. The pigeon grabbed her sleeve, flapping her wings frantically as she tried to pull Ellis south. "Stop that!"

Ellis batted the pigeon away. Wormy flew a few feet, then squawked again. "What are you trying to tell me?"

The pigeon looked toward the large cluster of theaters and chain restaurants that served as the hub of local tourism on Hollywood Boulevard and cooed again.

"Is that where the monster went?" Ellis asked.

Coo, coo.

"Do you know where Percy is?"

The pigeon ignored that question and winged in the indicated direction. Apparently, her friend was keeping an eye on things. *Cell networks go down, but birds are forever.*

Ellis ran the length of the boulevard, past dead neon signs. Falco easily kept up with her. Her muscles burned as she flashed like a UFO past the bronze stars on Hollywood Boulevard.

Her stomach twisted as she leapt over an abandoned Lime scooter and swerved around a trash can. The normal human bustle of the neighborhood, with street performers and bootleg superheroes and tourists wearing I Heart Hollywood shirts, had replaced by sirens and radio transmissions. But as she passed the El Capitan Theater and the Hollywood Masonic Temple and neared the ornate facade of the Chinese Theater, which was currently and ironically displaying a banner for the new Godzilla movie, the thunder of her footsteps was drowned out by screams.

A shadow passed over the sun, and she saw what they were screaming about. It wasn't an ordinary shadow. It was the torso of the beast, roiling with black tendrils, up so high on its haunches that it blocked half the light. It had gotten bigger and denser, and when it howled, its mouth dwarfed billboards advertising TV shows and a high-end Beverly Hills salon.

The monster took up so much of her attention that it was nearly a minute before she saw someone standing between the theater's ornate columns. Dirt had dulled the bright purple paisley of the man's shirt and his embroidered corduroy pants, but his posture was unmistakable.

It was Percy. He was at full height, arms outstretched to the monster in supplication. As Ellis sprinted toward him, she heard him mutter, "No way to treat your fellow citizens, Mr. Fuzzbutt." Was that what he had named it? Ellis would have gone for something intimidating, like Razortooth or Reaper or Oh, God, Please Don't Eat Me.

Percy was trying to talk to the monster. Of course he was. Open-minded about all creatures, Percy saw the monster not as a terrifying shadow beast but a new friend. However, this monster wasn't a whale or a king cobra or a leopard; it was a tangled amalgamation of rotting, angry souls. Ellis didn't think even Percy could befriend it.

"*Percy, no!*" Ellis screamed as she raced toward him.

He didn't look away from the shadow beast, but he heard her and responded, "Ellis?" The second syllable of her name was drowned out by a whine from the shadow beast.

The monster had Percy in its sights, limbs and jaws turned toward him. Percy might have interpreted that as an invitation for further communication, but Ellis only saw indifferent curiosity. Percy was not acting like other humans, and the monster was taking a good look at him before it discovered whether he tasted like other humans.

Sword high, Ellis jumped between Percy and the monster and skidded to a stop on the sidewalk.

"Don't be stupid, Percy." Her voice nearly broke with fear for him. She wiggled the shadow sword, which diverted the monster's attention. Unfortunately, it also made it angry. The whine turned into a roar.

"You'll never make new friends if you run into every encounter flapping a sword around," Percy stated. He was intent and serious, but he didn't look afraid.

"You'll never make new friends if you get eaten by a shadow beast," Ellis shot back, trying to feed her fighting prowess with her anger.

"I just need a few more minutes..." Percy protested. When the roar reached a crescendo, his voice faded.

"I could give you an eternity in the shadow realm, and it wouldn't help," Ellis hissed. "That thing isn't an animal. It's a magical construct, and it's going to kill you."

Taking careful, even steps, he moved behind her. "What?" His breathing hitched and accelerated.

"It's not an animal, not even a weird one. It was created with shadow magic from a bunch of angry drow souls."

"That explains why I've had trouble opening a line of communication," His voice had shot up into a higher register.

"Wormy helped me find you. She risked a lot by coming here. All your friends risked a lot, so if you won't do it for me, do it for them. Please, Percy, *run*. I'll hold off the monster."

The monster screeched, and a long, dark arm shot

down from the roof of the Chinese Theater. It stretched like a late evening shadow as it moved, slithering in front of the pitched pagoda roof and down the Godzilla banner. Ellis tried to step in front of it, but it knocked her away, spilling her face-down on the concrete. The air in its wake was so cold that she could see her panicked breath. She rolled to see black talons wrap around Percy's body.

Time seemed to skip, and before she was fully conscious of what she was doing, Ellis sprang to her feet with the sword out and sprinted toward the monster as it dragged her friend across the dirty sidewalk. Percy clawed at the monster's flesh, but his hands came away white with cold and failed to stop the monster's progress.

As the talon-tipped limb lifted Percy off the concrete, Ellis swung the sword in a wide arc, shouting as it made contact with the shadow flesh. The monster's skin seemed to have gotten thicker since she'd cut through its arm at the Hollywood Bowl, and the blade almost skidded off the scales. Ellis clenched her teeth and cut with as much power as she could muster. If she missed this chance, Percy would die.

The strange vibration between the void blade and the shadow flesh rattled Ellis' bones. When the roiling darkness tried to throw the blade away, she pressed down, and finally, Percy slipped from the inert talons and fell onto the concrete.

The shadow beast's scream drowned out anything she might have said, so she just watched as the hand clutching his body crystallized, the whirling black flesh freezing into static shapes. Ellis grabbed one of the creature's—fingers? Talons?—to pull it away from her friend, and it crumbled into dust so fine that it did not settle but hung in the air, a cloud of darkness surrounding them.

"I knew we were brought together for a reason," Percy wheezed. "Take more than a monster to snip the ties of Fate." After a thoughtful moment, he continued, "That sword might be able to do it, though."

"Are you okay?"

He shook his head. "Reckon I cracked something. Collarbone, mebbe."

Ellis nodded. "If you want to live longer, you'll have to deal with it."

She offered him a hand, and he gripped it lightly. As he pushed to his feet, Ellis shot a wave of cooling shadow magic down his arm and into his shoulder. Percy froze and gave her an odd look, but there was no time to react since the shadow beast had roared again and was winding up for another attack. Ellis half-pushed Percy behind her and stood her ground.

She had cut the monster's hand off, and it waved its stump in the air. There was no sign of blood, just a nub where the talons had been. The surface of the stump began to roil and three protrusions bubbled out, growing and extending until the hand reformed.

Dammit.

Ellis preferred it when sliced meat stayed sliced, but there would be no death by a thousand cuts here. She had to chop the creature's heart out.

The eyeless head turned toward her, and Ellis shivered when she saw the concentric rings of dripping black teeth. She raised the sword, and the monster shrieked. It paused for a moment, reared onto its back legs, and swiped at the roof beneath its feet. It made a wrecking ball noise and leapt into the hole it had just punched in the tiles.

The monster was inside the theater. She had made her choice, and she couldn't turn back now. The void sword shook in her hand, and not just from the cold.

"I might be able to provide some assistance." Falco was at her shoulder. "To slow the beast, if nothing else."

She couldn't afford to say no. "Then let's go."

The monster-infested building sounded like it was undergoing demolition. At least the people formerly inside had evacuated. Plaster rained on her head as she pushed through the embossed brass doors. It wasn't hard to follow the noise, and soon she was creeping into the main theater.

Moving between rows of rich red velvet seats, Ellis winced when she saw that large chunks of the ornately carved roof had collapsed. Ellis had hoped to use stealth, but the moment she entered the room, the monster turned to her. It must have a sense of smell or an affinity for shadow magic.

Ellis considered her options. The monster's limbs were flexible, and there would be no getting inside its guard. She had to avoid the gaping mouth as well. As far as she could tell, the monster didn't have bones, or if it did, she had cut through them as easily as its flesh. Her best bet would be to drop onto its back between its arms. Given the way it could stretch its body, it would grab her eventually, but she might have enough time to do what had to be done.

She told Falco the plan, and he nodded.

"You think it'll work?" she asked.

"No, but it is better than any alternative I can think of."

Spending thousands of years by himself had dulled his capacity for telling white lies.

"All right. Whatever you think you can do to help, do it now."

Light drained into the room from the house-sized hole the beast had created in the ceiling. Ellis pulled the grappling gun off her belt, testing her grip. She wasn't used to using it with her left hand, but she wasn't willing to let go of the sword. As she awkwardly aimed at the space above the monster's head, the circle of teeth swiveled toward her, and for a moment, she was mesmerized by the concentric jagged black rings. The grappling gun was going to pull her straight into those teeth.

"*Stop!*" someone screamed, and the monster froze. There was movement by her right shoulder as Falco picked his way between rows of velvet seats. When he reached the aisle, he stopped. The monster swiveled toward him and froze like someone had pushed the pause button on its body.

Falco's spine was very straight, and his hand was out. Was he using some arcane shadow magic? The shadow monster lowered its head toward the ancient drow.

"Friends, *stop!*" Falco repeated. "This violence is not necessary. You have served your people well. I beg you to rest. Rejoin the Mother and be at peace."

The monster was distracted, and she couldn't afford to lose this chance. She aimed at the hole in the ceiling, close to the edge. As she adjusted the gun's position, Ellis caught sight of a large white bird gyring across the opening. *One of Percy's?* There was no time to think about it because the bird disappeared.

Ellis pulled the trigger, and wire spooled out toward the roof. The second the grappling hook caught, she retracted the wire. The gun yanked her toward the ceiling, and she focused on the monster's back, trying to keep her eyes on the patch of shadow flesh between its arms. *Look at where you want to go, not at what you want to avoid.* Easier said than done when what you wanted to avoid was a hot-tub-sized maw of churning teeth.

As she sailed over the creature's head, Ellis dropped the gun's butt. The wire pulled her through the air with a metallic whoosh. She barely had enough time to grip the hilt of the void sword in both hands before the tip plunged into the monster's back.

Without the sword to anchor her, the monster would have thrown her off. She barely held on as the creature lunged toward Falco, its gnashing teeth producing a noise that, from this distance, was almost unbearable. Ellis had provided enough of a distraction for Falco to leap across the tops of the seats to get out of the monster's reach.

Ellis concentrated as the beast bucked and writhed beneath her, screaming in pain. Her flesh went cold wherever it touched the monster's body, and she found herself dancing from foot to foot as she struggled to maintain her grip. If she couldn't get this done quickly, she would freeze to death.

Seats snapped under the shadow beast's feet as it stamped and struggled. Bracing her feet against the creature's back, Ellis tightened her grip on the sword hilt and dragged it, slicing down what would have been the creature's spine if it had had a spine. No bones or organs appeared beneath the skin, just more dense shadow flesh.

The monster shrieked beneath her as she cut, and suddenly, the blade hit something more solid than its flesh. The sword bounced off the surface, and Ellis lost her grip.

The monster surged forward and she stumbled, arms cartwheeling as she fell across the creature's back. Before she tumbled several dozen feet to the twisted seats below, Ellis caught herself, digging one hand hard into the creature's back and grasping handfuls of its shifting flesh. Her hand froze to the point of pain, but Ellis ignored the bone-deep ache and squeezed the creature with her thighs as it reared, riding it like a rodeo bull from hell.

She needed a few seconds of stillness, just one or two, but the longer she stayed on its back, the more agitated the creature got. She was deeply jealous of professional bull riders, who only had to hang on for seven seconds.

She could imagine several horrible ways she could die. The monster might fling her into the air and eat her or throw her body to the floor with the force of a freight train. Maybe it would let her freeze to death on its back and then consume her like a popsicle. *Human and drow. Two flavors in one.*

There was a boom, and a light flickered on the massive screen. It took Ellis a moment to realize she was watching a movie's pre-show trailer. On the screen, Nicole Kidman was descending the steps of a movie theater in a shiny pinstriped suit.

Ellis glanced back. There was a dark figure in the booth. A projectionist who had decided to go down with the ship? Ellis sent out a silent prayer of gratitude.

The monster roared and raked the screen, and Ellis didn't waste the distraction. Half-frozen, she pulled herself up the creature's spine hand-over-hand until she could once again grip the shadow blade. Then she stared into the gash.

An opalescent gleam caught Ellis' eye. *There!* In the shadow monster's core was a black pearl the size of a fist. As she was about to plunge her arm into the slash, the monster made one final push to throw her off. Ellis felt like a marionette in a hurricane, barely hanging onto the hilt of the void sword as the creature flung her back and forth. The black pearl folded back into the wound.

Something in Ellis' shoulder tore, and a fireball of pain exploded in the joint. Her fingers slipped on the hilt as the monster shook again. When she was sure she'd be flung into Nicole Kidman's striped pantsuit, someone shouted from the top of the theater.

"*Hey!*" It was Charlie. Ellis remembered what he'd told her about working at a movie theater one summer when he was in college. He had turned on the projector to distract the monster, and now he was risking his life to buy Ellis time.

She was furious. Why hadn't he stayed with the other cops? What right did he have to risk his life for her? Her anger and adrenaline rushed in behind the pain in her shoulder, and the monster stopped bucking as it directed its attention at Charlie.

There was a thundering *pop-pop-pop* as Charlie discharged his gun into the monster's open mouth, to no apparent effect. A gurgle rose from the creature's throat, not of pain but of infernal laughter. The shadow monster pounced.

Charlie dove away as the shadow beast's front limbs

crashed down, and Ellis lost sight of him. The only indication that he was still alive was his cries of pain.

Ellis forgot about the pearl and pulled on the hilt of the sword, bracing her feet against it. It seemed to be frozen in the monster's flesh. She tugged again in desperation and rejoiced when the blade sprang free, but it was too late. The monster howled and leapt. In a blind panic, Ellis tightened her grip on the sword and slid down the frozen flesh onto a clear patch of aisle.

Charlie screamed again, and Ellis saw him. He was on his stomach, his right foot crushed below broken seats. As he tried to get to his knees, the monster blocked the sunlight streaming through the roof. It raised one of its arms above its head, the fist on the end expanding as the monster prepared to crush Charlie's head. Just before it struck, the monster's fist fell off. *What the hell?* Ellis glanced around, and through the triangle of space below the creature's legs, she saw the ancient dark elf.

Falco had cast a dissolution spell. He must have used an incredible amount of magic, and the shadow beast turned on him where he stood near the movie screen, the projector's light still flickering across the claw marks. The monster leapt toward the drow, eyestalks intent, mouth wide.

Eyes wide, Falco raised one hand in silent supplication as the maw descended and swallowed him whole. There was a flash of blue skin and a horrible crunch, and he was gone. A deep growl emerged from the monster's throat, an abyssal noise that chilled Ellis more than the beast's cold flesh. Overhead, a bird screamed.

Ellis had to get back on the monster's back. She had

seen the pearl, and all she had to do now was retrieve it. But Charlie was still in danger, crawling between rows of seats with an injured foot. Eating Falco seemed to have whetted the monster's hunger, and it now stalked toward Charlie.

The monster was in no hurry after its recent meal, and Ellis thought she might be able to leap back on its back. However, that would leave Charlie unprotected.

If you don't kill it now, it's going to eat the world. If she didn't save Charlie, what would the point of living be?

The monster raised a lazy forelimb in Ellis' direction, and she made her choice. She dove under the monster's belly, holding the sword aloft and putting her whole weight behind the cut. At the very least, it would draw the monster's attention back to her. Freezing black dust rained down on Ellis' head as the beast ululated in pain.

If she cut off its feet, it would grow new ones. That was a certainty, but if she moved fast enough, she could buy herself a few seconds. Maybe enough time to jump back on the monster's back and retrieve the pearl. Launching onto the arms of a theater seat, she picked her way across the chairs, zig-zagging down the monster's length. When it raised one taloned leg to crush her, she spun and sliced, cutting where it met the body.

The monster's weight came down on a leg that wouldn't support it. It wobbled, then surged forward with its arms out, and Ellis took a chance. Diving under the mass of the monster's body, she cut its other leg off, forcing the void sword through the dense flesh until the blade swung free.

A howl pounded her eardrums, loud and high. It was

more of a chorus. She couldn't pick out the individual voices, but she could feel the reedy threads bound together into a single, awful noise. She was fighting for them too, she remembered—the souls who had been bound to this monstrous half-existence.

The nobility of this thought was cut short when the monster's severed leg dissolved into dust and its body plummeted straight onto Ellis. She dropped to the floor in a row of seats, but it only helped a little. The monster was heavy, and the rows of seats on either side of her crumbled and pressed down on her back. Her sword arm was stretched out in front of her, pinned beneath a mound of flesh that was colder than ice.

It was like being trapped in a blast chiller. Ellis shivered until her energy hit a wall, and stopped being able to move. A deep sense of peace washed over her, her fear and adrenaline dissolving into euphoria.

Oh, no, you fucking don't. Not today. If she was going to die in a fight with a limb-regrowing shadow beast, she was going to do it bellowing and waving a sword. She was going to be eaten, not pressed to death by frozen meat.

Ellis sent a silent cry for help to the sword. She tried to tighten her fingers around it, but they were frozen on the hilt, flesh white. *Please. Please help.*

The blade twitched where it lay flat on the floor. It jumped once, twice, then turned on edge and violently jerked up into the belly of the beast. The monster screamed and rolled, and the sword, still buried in the black flesh, left Ellis' hand. She grabbed for it, but the monster was moving away.

On the plus side, she had room to move. Forcing her sluggish limbs to respond, she crawled to her feet.

The monster had rolled over and was pawing at the sword embedded in its belly. Its legs were regrowing, but they were half-formed nubs, useless for standing. Its back rested between two rows of seats, and Ellis could see the cut she'd made. There was a foot or so of space between the body and the floor.

It would have to be enough. Dropping onto her back, Ellis inched beneath the writhing monster, wincing every time it rolled. Soon, she was under the beast, and she could see the seamless abyss of a gash.

The pearl! The gleaming dark sphere caught her eye, even in the low light. Ellis reached toward the gap, but the monster rolled away, thrashing in pain.

Wait for it.

She took a deep breath, hand poised. And when the monster rolled back over her, she plunged her hand into the wounded flesh, teeth gritted against the cold. She had lost all feeling in her hand, but she forced her fingers to curl around the smooth surface of the pearl and ripped it free of the monster's chest.

It was warm. Its surface was frictionless, and it made the dark, cramped space glow with a lustrous purple light. The monster above Ellis stilled and went silent, and she heard voices calling her from the theater beyond the mass of flesh.

Other voices produced an ancient sing-song chorus in a language Ellis didn't speak but could somehow understand. It sang of a profound sorrow, the kind of wrenching tragedy that could plunge a person into a dark pit. The music was pierced with blood and rage. It was a cry to battle, to take up bows and magic against the humans.

I'm human.

The pearl pulsed, its song louder and shriller. On the attack, the wails thrummed against her eardrums, and the smooth surface was hotter as it vibrated in her hands.

Cut out the part of you that is human, it cried to her.

Ellis growled. She had spent many years at war against herself without positive results. She wasn't going to let some stupid monster pearl tell her what to do now. Rocking her body back and forth, she wiggled free from beneath the monster, pearl clutched in her hands.

When she reached the sunlight, the pearl was almost too hot to hold. She needed to destroy it. Without its heart, the monster was an unmoving black lump in the middle of the theater. Ellis climbed over it, the icy flesh affecting her feet and her breath making soft clouds in the cold air.

This time, the void sword came free easily. As she drew it from the monster's torso, chunks of black flesh briefly clung to the blade before disappearing into it as if they'd been vacuumed up by a great force.

Now.

Ellis tossed the pearl up and grabbed the sword with both hands. The blade was a black arc, moving so fast that the immediate vicinity fell into twilight. Then the leading edge caught the falling pearl and bit through its lustrous shell.

The pearl exploded. Millenia of pressure and anger surged out, sending opalescent shrapnel in every direction. Ellis hit the shadow monster's corpse, and it turned to dust beneath her.

Purple light exploded through the theater, glimmering off every reflective surface. It made the sunlight coming through the hole in the ceiling above look dingy by comparison. Lying on her back in a pile of freezing dust, Ellis watched as glowing violet orbs careened around the room in confusion. Those were the freed drow souls, Ellis realized. There were hundreds of them, eroded by years of anger and grief until they were indistinguishable from one another.

Except one, a tall column of blue light standing at the monster's head.

Ellis pushed herself into a sitting position, watching a familiar tall shape phase in and out. Falco. He'd spent thousands of years alone, and when he'd finally returned to the world, he'd had so little time. However, he looked peaceful. The column bowed, emanating a sensation of warm gratitude that eased Ellis' exhaustion, then straightened and drifted forward. Ellis realized that Falco's soul was moving toward the void sword. When the column of light met the blade, it changed from black to purple.

All the souls careening through the glittering, ruined theater drifted toward her, floating toward the void blade from all directions like a dandelion puffing in reverse. The void blade kept pulsing with purple magic, the color growing deeper with each addition. Finally, only a single violet wisp was left.

Ellis walked to meet it, and when the last thread disappeared inside the blade, the sharp length flashed with purple light and folded in on itself with a sucking noise. The void stitched itself up with a crackling boom, leaving only air. Ellis was left holding the black metal hilt, which warmed in her hand.

The ground rumbled. The Mother Beneath had welcomed her people home.

A hand descended on Ellis' shoulder, and she jumped.

"Whoa," Charlie wheezed.

Ellis wrapped her arms around him, realizing how cold she was. She began to shiver violently, a good sign, and mournfully looked at his face. "I'd k-k-k-kiss you, but I'm afraid-d-d-d I'd b-b-b-ite your tongue off." Her teeth wouldn't stop chattering.

"I have questions." Charlie glanced at the six-inch-deep pile of black dust at their feet. "You can answer them after you warm up."

After Ellis nodded, he pointed her toward the exit. Something whistled overhead, a curious sound she barely heard over the ringing in her ears. Then the ceiling exploded. Ellis froze at the unmistakable roar of a mortar blast. She glanced dumbly at a sedan-sized chunk of plummeting concrete.

At least I saved the world first, she thought remotely. Just before impact, however, the concrete dissolved. Ellis blinked, then turned to Charlie. Her shadow magic powers were almost entirely depleted, but she had enough magic left to see the purple dregs in Charlie's hands. He had blasted it away. "I g-g-guess you're n-n-not afraid of dissolution magic anymore."

"I'm petrified, but I'm more afraid of losing you."

She wished they had time to stare longingly into each other's eyes, but he wasn't looking at her anymore. He pulled her toward the back of the building. He was clearly in pain, and Ellis suspected his right foot was broken, but his adrenaline wouldn't allow him to stop. He moved quickly despite the injury.

As they reached the lobby, a second mortar exploded behind them. Charlie reached for his walkie-talkie. *"Liza! Call off the cavalry. The monster is dead."*

There was a long silence. "Charlie? Thank God," Liza sounded immensely relieved despite the static. "I'll see what I can do, but I'm not running this show."

Great. Not only had they killed an ancient shadow beast, but they might have to escape while dodging friendly fire. Assuming the Army counted as friendly, which was as up in the air as your average ballistic missile.

Ellis reached for her bottle of potion and unscrewed the lid. When she tipped it into her mouth, however, nothing happened. What the hell? It was still heavy. She noted the condensation on the bottle and realized it had frozen solid. "Shit!" She showed it to Charlie. "I hope you can turn both of us invisible."

Liza crackled back on. "Charlie?"

"Yeah."

"There's bombers incoming. You gotta get out of there."

"Copy that." Charlie grabbed Ellis' hand. "Let's go."

"Where?" Ellis asked. She put her hands over her eyes. She was warming up, but that was how her body was spending all of its energy. She wondered if she'd be able to walk out of the building, much less run. "I can't, Charlie."

"Yes, you fucking *can*." He didn't sound sympathetic. He sounded furious. "I'll carry you if I have to."

"Your foot's broken." Ellis pointed. Charlie was

balancing on his left foot, hand braced against the wall for support.

"Well, then you'd better buck up."

Ellis started to cry. She felt ridiculous as the tears made muddy pathways through the black dust clinging to her skin. Why did she always have to fight both sides at the same time?

"Hey!" Charlie sounded sympathetic and also afraid.

"I'm fine. I'm with you. We'll do whatever we have to."

The walkie-talkie crackled. "Charlie? They've got the front surrounded, but not a lot of DRI support there. The back's more sparsely populated, but they've got lightsilk and guns."

"Where are you?"

"In the back, but we're way behind the front lines. Whatever you do, you'd better do it quick."

The distant noise of jet engines got louder. "Thanks, Liza. For everything." Ellis didn't like how much it sounded like a goodbye. "What do you think? Guns or lightsilk?"

Ellis blew out a breath. "Guns. It has to be guns."

"We can't just fling a door open. They'll see it and start shooting."

"If we can get to the roof, we can get outside without raising suspicion."

"We can also get up close and personal with the bombs they're about to drop on us." Charlie sighed. "I guess that's a risk we'll have to take. Come on."

Ellis stumbled toward the nearest staircase, ignoring Charlie's whimpers of pain when he put his weight on his right foot. She would spoon-feed him all the mushroom painkillers in the world once they got out of there.

A door next to a broken popcorn machine led to a utility stairwell, and Ellis and Charlie moved as quickly as they could up several flights. When they reached a door that led outside, the jets were visible overhead. They stuck to the parts of the building where the monster hadn't caved the roof in. As Ellis tried to find a place where they could climb down, she saw a glittering metal object stuck to a caved-in edge of the roof. Hobbling over, she grabbed her grappling gun.

"*Charlie!*" she shouted. He limped over.

The planes were dangerously close, and as Charlie reached her, a bomb whizzed down at the far end of the building, and half of it exploded.

"*Grab my waist!*" Ellis yelled.

Charlie's warm arms wrapped around her. It was a nice feeling. *I should flee certain death more often,* she thought as she aimed the grappling gun at the balcony of the apartment complex behind the theater. The hook whizzed toward the other building and caught a balcony rail with a satisfying click.

"Hold on tight." Ellis pressed the retraction button, grabbing the handle. The grappling gun yanked them off the roof with incredible force, and they careened toward the apartment building. They were going to slam into the wall with a fair amount of force, so Ellis braced her feet, aiming for an expanse of tinted window.

Her boots shattered the glass and they sailed into an empty apartment, rolling across the floor amid a rain of shards. Her hip was cold and wet. She was afraid she'd been injured, but when she checked, the bottle of shadow magic potion had shattered, and the rapidly warming liquid was draining onto the floor.

Ellis cursed. "I'm out of shadow magic." She checked herself for injuries, then turned to do the same for Charlie. "You'll have to take care of both of us."

He was tearing a piece of his shirt off to make a bandage for a long cut on his arm, but he nodded. After a few moments of recovery, Ellis pulled them through the empty living room toward the door.

His walkie-talkie crackled. "Charlie?" Liza asked tentatively. "Charlie, there's a unit—" Someone in the background screamed an order, and a fight broke out before the radio went dead.

"Liza. There's a unit *where?*" Charlie shouted, then shook his head. "That's not good."

"No, but we can't stay here."

Ellis wasn't willing to risk the elevator, so she and Charlie went to the staircase. Charlie's adrenaline was ebbing, and the pain from his foot had sent him into the first stages of shock. Ellis didn't like how clammy his skin was, and after the second time his eyes lost focus and he nearly fell over the banister, she slid under his arm to support him as they moved down.

When a door opened below and the heavy footsteps skipped up the stairs, Ellis froze.

"You have to turn us invisible!" Ellis' heart sank when she looked at him. His skin had gone from pale to gray, and he was struggling to stay conscious. He was too exhausted to respond, so he closed his eyes and stretched out his hands. The fluorescent lighting in the stairwell was bright, and he was too weak to collect the meager shadows at the edges of the shaft. He tried again as the pounding footsteps drew closer.

"Ellis, I can't," he said, voice rasping. He swayed on his feet and sank, pulling Ellis down onto the step. Shit. She didn't want to die under fluorescent lighting.

A wave of soldiers fell upon them. The air sparkled with lightsilk, and exhaustion gripped her. Her consciousness was a hard knot buried in the depths of her body. In the bright world above, she was in pain, crisscrossed with lightsilk netting, her skin a burning checkerboard, but she wasn't up there anymore. Not really.

Ellis closed her eyes against the light, her body slumping. As she sank into darkness, barely feeling the hands that relieved her of the grappling gun and scabbard and secured her wrists behind her. Everything was cool and dim. The version of her that was stumbling down the stairs was far away.

"He's out. This guy's foot is shredded meat," someone above her said. It was like someone was speaking to her through a tube from far away. "He's dressed like a cop, but I can't find a badge."

She was so tired. It was dark and cool where her spirit was, with a smooth stone floor below her, the ceiling a distant vault. She was in a cavern, she realized. Deep underground, the air around her cool and redolent with the smell of growing mushrooms.

And she wasn't alone. Ellis blinked and saw a dark shape moving toward her, a shrouded figure clad in veils woven from shadows. When the person spoke, her voice was as warm and hard as a hot poker. Was this another hallucination sent to her by the ring? She looked down, but wherever she was, her hands were bare.

Ellis

Realization dawned on her when the Mother Beneath spoke her name. She inhaled and looked more closely at the figure. But her eyes slid away from the layers of shadows. The Mother Beneath was not meant to be seen.

There were more figures behind the Mother. Pale purple and blue shapes, hundreds of them. She recognized only one, a tall blue man standing behind the Mother's right shoulder. It was Falco. The other souls had regained their individuality, and she was able to pick out the faces of the men, women, and children.

When the Mother spoke, a dark mist flowed from her mouth and wrapped around Ellis' head, filling her mouth and nose and ears with mist and delivering her words directly to Ellis' brain.

You've done well, child.

"You're not angry?" Ellis choked out. The shadow beast had been born of the Mother's rage, and Ellis had killed it. Maybe gods didn't think like that.

You corrected an error I made a long time ago. I am reunited with my people.

"Am I dead?" Ellis whispered. The following pause was not reassuring.

Do you wish to be dead?

The voice filled Ellis' body, and she looked down at her hands. They were a ghostly semi-transparent lilac. Then they solidified and went back to her normal skin color. As Ellis watched, her skin flickered in and out of existence, and she understood. The Mother was offering her a choice.

A chance to rest, a chance for her spirit to sink into the earth and return to a place of cool darkness and shadow magic.

"I'm tired." Tears welled in her eyes.

Then she thought about Charlie. He wasn't here with her. Maybe he was alive and well. Her heart leapt at that hope. Maybe he had gone to a different afterlife. He'd grown up Catholic, so maybe he was making small talk with Saint Peter at the Pearly Gates. He was only a small part drow.

Ellis could stay here and rest, but the Mother Beneath would allow her to return to the world if she wished. The weight of the choice overwhelmed her. There was blinding light and heat and pain in the world above. Possibly war between the humans and the drow. There was also Charlie.

She had no choice.

The Mother Beneath laughed. It sounded like an earthquake, and it vibrated in Ellis' bones.

Very well, child. I will send you back above. But I think you have earned a small gift.

The Mother Beneath flowed forward over the smooth stone, and Ellis was embraced by cool hands. Pain trickled back into her body, and the ceiling was pierced with light. The Mother's cool power relieved the renewed burning, and when she leaned forward, Ellis felt the Mother's lips on her own. She was blinded, plunged into bottomless dark peace.

Her mouth filled with shadow magic. The cool river of power flowed into her, rushing toward her hands and feet and splitting into rivulets that filled her fingers and toes.

Ellis' heart leapt as a well that had been empty refilled to overflowing.

"Thank you!" Tears rained down her cheeks. When she brushed them away, she saw that the salty streaks glowed purple. "What do you want me to do?"

As you saw today, I made unwise decisions the last time I meddled in the human world. You must pick your course of action for yourself.

Ellis shivered. It was a tremendous responsibility, but she was fortified by the knowledge that this peace awaited her at the end. She nodded. "I understand." She would have to make that true.

I will see you again, Ellis Burton. But not for a long time, I think. The Mother receded into the crowd of spirits arrayed at her back.

Ellis opened her eyes and screamed in pain. Soldiers surrounded her, although her view was impeded by the glittering net covering her eyes. The lines of fire burned, but they did not consume the newfound shadow magic flowing through her veins.

Ellis screamed in rage and sent a wave of dissolution magic out from every inch of her body. The lightsilk dissolved into glittering dust, and the soldier pressing her shoulder against the staircase yanked his hand away as the magic ate through his tactical gloves and took off a layer of skin beneath.

Angry, in pain, and possessing a level of shadow magic she had never before had, Ellis got to work. The subsequent fight went by in flashes of punches and kicks punctuated by outpourings of gleaming purple power.

Her first wave of shadow magic split the soldiers'

machine guns in half. One got off a round first, but the remaining bullets dissolved against a glowing purple shield, gone before they traveled more than a foot.

Ellis yanked the lightsilk net off Charlie, ignoring the burning streaks that rose on her hands when she grabbed the fabric. As she tossed the net aside, she sent a wave of healing magic into his foot. It wouldn't repair the tissues, but it would buy him enough time to escape.

"Ellis?" Charlie murmured tentatively. Ellis looked down and saw that her hands were rippling with purple magic. Awe and fear commingled in his eyes.

"I'll explain later." Another wave of soldiers fell upon them. Her first kick knocked one soldier into another, and they both tumbled down the stairs. When she grabbed Charlie to pull him over the bodies, another soldier seized her. Bone snapped under her hand as she struck his arm away.

As she descended the steps, magic flowed into Ellis' hands from the shadows at the corners of the stairs, the dark gaps below the soldiers' bodies, and the darkness under her feet and behind her eyes. Ellis cocooned herself and Charlie in a thick, cool blanket of invisibility as they descended to the ground floor.

"What the hell is happening?" Charlie asked. Her healing magic had improved his skin color and pain levels, but he was still dazed.

"I kissed a god," Ellis explained.

Charlie looked like he was about to laugh but stopped when he saw her face. "Lucky god," he remarked after a long pause.

Ellis grinned, but she only had time to peck him on the cheek.

Soldiers had occupied the building's lobby, and it took Ellis and Charlie a few minutes to weave through them. Floating on a cloud of shadow magic, Ellis felt invulnerable. When two soldiers slipped through the automatic doors a few minutes later, Ellis and Charlie were behind them.

"Their door protocol is shit," she told Charlie as they moved away from the building. She pulled them into an out-of-the-way alcove in front of a boarded-up Persian ice cream store, and they rested in the shade for a moment.

"What happened in there?"

"It's hard to explain."

She looked at the Chinese Theater. A thin line of smoke curled up into the flat blue sky. Ellis hadn't planned farther ahead than killing the monster since she had not believed she would survive that. What now?

The doors of the apartment complex opened. Ellis sprang to her feet as twenty soldiers, mostly men, surged out of the building, but she was still invisible, and they ignored her. Their attention was focused on a crowd of people turning onto the Boulevard from the north. A group of drow walking openly down the asphalt.

"Look!" Ellis directed Charlie's attention down the street, and her stomach made a tumbling pass when she saw that Connor and Ilva were at the head of the delegation. Connor held a long metal pole embossed with drow symbols bearing a white crystal silk banner aloft. As the drow walked, Connor waved it in a slow arc. As he passed a light post, he held up a hand, and the drow stopped. He continued forward. Ellis and Charlie crept toward the Army's defensive line, not wanting to put themselves between two armies. Ellis heard one of the men say, "I think that's their leader."

An officer nodded. "We might not get another chance. Ready the snipers."

No. Ellis frantically looked around and saw a shadow of a figure on top of a nearby roof. She would never make it in time, but she had to try.

As Ellis was about to sprint off, someone spoke. "No!" a man said.

Ellis turned to look.

"General Jarwell!" one of the soldiers called. The gold bars on the man's shoulder gleamed.

"Let's hear them out," the general suggested.

"Should I delegate an envoy?" a sergeant asked.

"No. I'll go," the general replied.

He straightened and was about to step toward the drow when one of his soldiers stopped him. "Excuse me, sir, but you need to look at this."

"Is that a fucking TikTok, soldier?" the general asked. He sounded angry.

"Yes, sir. It's the only thing showing on every social media network."

"I thought we were the only ones with comms. The cell networks are down. How the hell are people watching TikToks?"

The soldier sounded nervous. "Sir, someone appears to have hacked into a military satellite and brought some comms back online."

Ellis frowned and pulled her phone out of her pocket.

The screen was shattered, and she winced as she sliced her finger on the broken glass.

She renewed the muffling spell around her and Charlie. "Is your phone working?" she asked.

When Charlie checked, his screen was flooded with messages. He scrolled through several apps, and after a moment, he pulled up a video. As he pressed play, a dark-haired woman leapt onto a monster's back.

"Oh, shit! That's me!" Ellis exclaimed. "Who took this?"

It looked like drone footage shot from overhead. After it played for a few minutes, her question was answered when a bird's cry interrupted the sound. *"Mariner?"* Ellis cried in disbelief. She remembered the squawks she'd heard and the flash of white feathers during the fight.

Percy hadn't abandoned them. He had sent Mariner to help them, not with a bomb or gun but with a camera. Now he was showing the world what they had achieved.

The video showed everything from Charlie's projector ruse to Falco's sacrifice to the final killing slice through the pearl. She glanced at the comments. Some insisted that the video was fake, but most were positive.

This chick is badass.

Slay, queen.

Ellis smiled. There were a lot of things she enjoyed about being a vigilante, like kicking asshole's faces in, but she'd never gotten much in the way of public appreciation. She stared at the screen, rapt until Charlie gently tugged it away from her.

"Please don't become a vigilante influencer." They were well-muffled, but Charlie kept his voice low.

"Is that an option? I'd have to have a cool name."

"'Ellis Burton' is plenty cool."

There was movement near the windows of a nearby gift shop. The streets had previously been abandoned, but a small group of humans had collected near the building, eyeing Connor and Ilva. They were taking photos and recording videos.

"Shit!" One of the soldiers directed the general's attention to the onlookers.

"Well, we can't shoot them now." The general sounded pleased.

"What do we do?"

"Something radical."

"Sir?"

"Let's go say hello. Do we have a white flag?"

The soldier looked around. Several of the soldiers were wearing thin lightsilk coverings over their body armor. When the general saw those, he shook his head. "You're wearing magical objects! *Take them off!*"

One was affixed to the top of a broom someone rushed out with.

The general unholstered his sidearm and nodded to an aide to bear their sweaty parlay banner. Together, they marched forward.

"I think it's time we join this party," Ellis told Charlie.

There was a moment of confusion when Ellis and Charlie popped into existence next to Connor, Ilva, and the general. The military contingent shouted, but Ellis and

Charlie had placed the general between them and the guns, and he held up a hand.

The general blinked when Charlie popped into view. "Charlie Morrissey."

"General," Charlie acknowledged. "How's your ferret?"

Ellis frowned in confusion. Was that cop or military slang?

The general's eyebrows went up fractionally. "His hair grew back."

"When we were locked up, Percy helped the general with a ferret problem," Charlie told Ellis.

"Percy does that."

As if it had heard them, a large white bird shrieked overhead, circling the parlay.

"Is that the bird that took the video?" the general asked.

"I think so," Ellis stated.

He nodded. "Where is our animal-loving friend?"

Ellis shook her head. "I don't know. He was pretty pissed off about the rain of fish."

"Not too pissed off to come through in a pinch, though."

"That's true."

"We have *quite* a situation on our hands," the general said. "I wasn't thrilled about you robbing a military weapons depot, but I was pleased to see that you made good use of that sword. I won't pretend to know what happened in the theater with that monster, but it looks pretty dead in the video, which is the most important thing."

"It is," Ellis confirmed.

"Interestingly, you captured a video of both humans

and MECs..." He paused when Ellis and Connor winced. "I'm sorry. That's not the right word. You'll have to forgive me. I'm more of a soldier than a diplomat."

Connor nodded appreciatively. "Drow. We're called drow or dark elves."

"We got one of the *drow* on video helping this lady defeat the thing."

"His name was Falco," Ellis' voice cracked. Now was not the time to mention that he had also summoned the monster way back when. That could wait.

"The American people owe Falco a debt of gratitude," the general asserted, then turned to Connor and Ilva. "Are you two authorized to speak for your community?"

They looked at each other. "Truthfully, the drow leadership has been thrown into chaos. Many of our elders recently died." He didn't mention Lola's short-lived coup. "But I believe that I can ensure peace in the short term if peace is on the table."

"Peace is always on the table," the general growled, then sighed. "Or that's the way it should be."

"How things should be is not always the way things are," Connor countered. "Are *you* authorized to speak for *your* people?"

"I'm authorized to speak for the ones with the big guns," the general agreed drily.

"That is our first concern," Ilva asserted gravely.

"There has been...contact before. Between humans and the drow," Connor continued.

"Little of it good in recent years," Ilva added.

"How much do you know about the DRI?" Ellis asked the general.

Jarwell shook his head. "A little through Chan. After we captured your crew," he nodded at Charlie, "Chan gave us some operational information. Pretty thin on details, though. At some point, a top-top-top secret project becomes too secret to do anyone any good."

"It did not do the drow any good," Ilva hissed.

"My father and brother were held captive and tortured by the DRI." Ellis touched her father's arm. Connor straightened to his full height.

"You two..." the general looked from Ellis to Connor, taking in their features. "He's your dad?" the general asked Ellis, nodding at Connor.

"My mother is Claire Burton. She worked for the DRI for a long time," Ellis explained.

"Huh."

Their expressions conveyed that the love story had not had a happy ending.

"You're half-drow as well?" Jarwell asked Charlie.

"Er, no." Charlie fidgeted.

"That's a story for another time," Ellis interjected.

"Hmmm."

Ellis peered at the soldiers behind the general. While they were talking, a bristling array of guns and artillery had been aimed away from the Chinese Theater and toward the drow.

"Let's talk terms," the general suggested.

Ilva's eyebrows arched. "Let me be very clear. We are not here to surrender. We will not walk blindly into torture and captivity." The general looked offended, but their faces were so serious that he nodded.

Ilva continued, "You *could* harm us. You could set fire to

our homestead and decimate our families, but the drow are neither weak nor defenseless. How long could you stand against an invisible enemy that can melt walls and flesh with the twitch of a finger? You can only manufacture so much lightsilk. We plead not for mercy but for peace."

Ilva looked ferocious. Ellis had thought her father would assume the role of elder speaker after Katya's death. Now, she wondered if the staff would pass to Ilva.

"The Army is used to being the big dog in the fight. Also, it's been a long time since we've seen battle on American soil." He sighed, long and deep. "If you're willing, there's someone I think you should meet."

"Another soldier?" Connor asked.

"Please don't take us to Chan again," Ellis pleaded. They had gone to that well one too many times.

The general shook his head. "I wasn't talking about Chan."

The general held his walkie-talkie to his face and pressed a button. "Commander? Yeah, it's Jarwell. I need you to get me the President."

"The President of what?" Ellis asked.

Jarwell frowned at her. "The United States, kid."

Ellis and Charlie exchanged looks. This was going to be interesting.

CHAPTER THIRTEEN

Ellis had been in plenty of tight spots, and she was no stranger to risking her life. She'd felt fear before, for herself or her family or for Charlie, but that danger had been personal and limited in scope.

As she facilitated diplomatic negotiations between the humans and the drow during the next few weeks, she had to develop a new kind of bravery. She was responsible for much more than her life now. One misstep and the consequences for the drow and humans could be catastrophic. Too much caution was as dangerous as too much boldness.

She lived in constant terror. She lost weight she couldn't afford to lose even though Charlie and Trissa constantly plied her with tunnel bars.

The American government had commandeered a group of cabins that were normally used as a summer camp. Bordering the Angeles National Forest to the north, the cabins and surrounding area were designated as a neutral territory for conducting negotiations. The most significant concession Ellis had won so far was that the border was left open to the forest, allowing the drow to freely travel back and forth from the Homestead. They were currently prohibited from mingling with the human population without a police or military escort, although General Jarwell insisted that that was for their protection.

Best of all, Percy had reappeared. He was still giving Connor the silent treatment, but Ellis hoped they would eventually repair their relationship. He and Rose had joined the drow delegation on the drow side. Rose contributed diplomatically useful dirt on a significant number of prominent men in Los Angeles, and even when she didn't have insider information, she was exceptionally good at reading people.

The drow delegation had taken over a cluster of six cabins. Sebastian had resumed her swimming lessons in the camp pool. Ellis didn't think she'd ever be graceful in the water, but she could dog paddle now. She had gone for a swim this evening before sunset, and now she was on the porch of her cabin, occasionally glancing out at the water as she read the peace treaty on her computer screen for the umpteenth time. Her eyes ached.

"You're not going to find any mistakes our lawyers didn't." Charlie put a hand on her shoulder, then, ignoring her protests, he gently closed her laptop screen. They'd gotten support from interesting quarters. A legal firm that represented the Tongva tribe in Los Angeles had offered the drow their services pro bono. Adept at navigating complex legal negotiations involving tribal sovereignty on American soil, they had proven to be critical in the subsequent negotiations. They had signed off on the peace treaty, but Ellis still wanted to do her part.

There was a coo from the porch railing. Wormy scratched at the wood. Apparently, she agreed with Charlie that Ellis was working too hard.

"We should go to bed," Charlie suggested.

"I'm not going to be able to sleep until everything's signed."

"Who said anything about sleep?" Charlie asked. There was enough starlight that she could see his wide grin.

Ellis took his hand, and they went inside. They had been chaotically busy, but they had still found private moments together. Charlie had finally opened up about his worries. What if their age difference was too big, and what if it got bigger as they aged at different rates?

"If you don't want to waste your youth on me, Charlie, you just have to say so," Ellis had insisted. It had taken him by surprise. So did her pointing out that his newfound shadow magic might have come with other side effects.

Charlie's fears were not powerful enough to keep them apart. Over the past several weeks, they had fallen into a companionable partnership. Despite his grinning insinuation, she fell asleep in his arms that night.

Ellis' shadow magic was stronger than ever. So strong that she would spend a long time exploring its limits. It was her responsibility to develop her skills to the greatest extent.

She had mostly discussed the matter with Trissa. Trissa was also the only person aside from Charlie that Ellis had told about her conversation with the Mother Beneath. The young drow had listened to the story with awe and curiosity.

"She didn't give you instructions about what to do here, did she?" Trissa had asked.

"I wish." That would have been much easier.

The next day dawned gray but bright. The overcast was a boon for the drow, and Ellis enjoyed the dance of shadow magic beneath the clouds as she drank too much coffee on the porch.

"Ambassador Burton?" someone said from the doorway. It was a female military attaché about Ellis' age. Connor Burton was standing at the woman's shoulder, which was clearly making her nervous. Her face was calm, but her eyes were worried.

"I'm still in my pajamas," Ellis looked down at the blue-and-green plaid flannel. "Would you please call me Ellis?"

"No, ma'am," the attaché declined, although the side of her mouth twitched up at the request. "When you're ready, I'm here to escort you to the signing."

The Foreign Service had loaned the drow a protocol officer named Corbin McMasters, who had helped Ellis and her family organize the ceremonial aspects of the peace treaty ceremony. McMasters was an energetic man who would have been an event planner if he hadn't been such a serious person. He was in the cabin when Ellis came out of her room, waiting to check her over.

Connor and Ilva were wearing traditional drow clothing. Ilva was draped in her elder speaker's garb and carried the metal staff of office, as Ellis had predicted. Connor, Landon, and Trissa were also present, along with representatives from the rangers and the miners. These included families with young children who considered the whole thing a fantastic adventure.

Ellis had struck a balance between drow and human clothing. Since she looked human, she wanted to remind everyone that she was also part drow. She had opted for a loose crystal silk pantsuit in drow purple, embroidered with fungal whorls. She applied a sedate shade of lipstick and turned to Charlie. "How do I look?"

"Impressive," Charlie said. He was wearing his full LAPD dress uniform. He'd been reinstated, although removed from Homicide. That had stung, even though he had been put in charge of the new Drow Affairs division.

Wormy squawked appreciatively, preening her feathers. Even the odd-eyed pigeon had cleaned up for the occasion.

Ellis hoped that Wormy was a name and not a diagnosis. She joined the rest of her family. Landon looked the most out-of-place, picking at his stiff drow collar and bouncing from one foot to the other whenever Trissa wasn't looking at him. As part of the treaty process, Landon and Connor had both given testimony to the Armed Forces Committee of the House of Representatives, detailing what had been done to them at the DRI. They had both been quieter than usual since those meetings.

Claire had disappeared, probably gone to ground with help from one of the international contacts she'd made over the years. Ellis had been too busy to think about it much, and when she did, it was a familiar absence.

Maybe her mother would resurface one day. Although she was gone, she was not forgotten. A few weeks after the shadow monster had been defeated and things in the city had calmed down, Ellis had gotten a letter with the key to a safe deposit box.

In it, she had found a laptop and several external hard

drives full of information. The hard drives contained all of Claire's research, including the top-top-secret work she'd done for the DRI. Ellis hadn't shared the information with anyone except Percy, who was combing through the data at a leisurely pace.

She'd insisted on a full pardon for the animal psychic. That had been the hardest concession to obtain, but some behind-the-scenes maneuvering from General Jarwell had secured it.

Percy had tried to weasel out of the signing ceremony, but Ellis wanted him there. After promising him that several police horses and a bomb-sniffing dog would also be in attendance, she wore down his resolve. Now he was waiting outside the cabin, fidgeting with the bowtie on an eggplant-colored suit.

"You look…"

"As sharp as a blade forged from endless night?" Percy asked with a grin.

"I was going to say you look like yourself. Good, but like yourself." Rose was beside him, looking shattering with waves of her red hair falling around a high-necked green gown. She had been instrumental in securing the support of a range of Southern California politicians. Ellis guessed she was going to have a second career as a diplomat.

Ellis raised an eyebrow at the smug smile on Percy's face. "What is it?"

"The invisible threads of Fate pulled us toward one another, Ellis girl. I believe it was for this very reason."

Ellis snorted. "That's 'Ambassador Girl' to you."

He ignored that and continued, "I thought Fate was

pulling me to you, and vice versa. Maybe its invisible threads were pulling us both here."

Ellis thought about that. Then she thought about what the Mother Beneath had told her. "I don't think so. This isn't Fate. We created it, and we have to keep creating things like this. We can't just wait for unseen forces to yank us to our destinies."

Percy shrugged, still smiling. "Mebbe they just tug us into the general area on occasion."

"Well, they'd better start tugging, or we're going to miss the ceremony."

The ceremony was scheduled to take place at dusk, a metaphorical nod to the meeting of light and dark—a nice touch that McMasters had thought of. He was with the rest of the drow contingent, waiting in a large central area between the clustered cabins.

The protocol officer fussed over them, straightening collars and menacing them with a handheld garment steamer, oblivious to the murderous looks Ilva was giving him.

As he pulled a small container of hair gel from his pocket and vigorously applied it to a loose strand of black hair, Ellis heard a noise from the forest, a faint rustle of branches. She froze, then turned toward the sound. There was a soft twang, and Ellis' shoulder burned. Corbin glanced from the bleeding red line on her arm to the arrow buried in the nearby soil in shock.

"It came from the trees!" Ellis screamed, grabbing McMasters and pulling him toward the nearest building. She zeroed in on the forest as she ran, listening for the

sound of a bow being drawn. She heard shouts and a loud thump.

She reached the building and peered out at the forest. Two figures were visible. Ellis caught a flash of a pinched drow face before Security swarmed them. Who was the other person? They looked human.

Ellis told McMasters to stay where he was and ran over to the security detail with her family at her heels. Mirelle was screeching in a pair of lightsilk handcuffs—in anger, though, rather than pain. Their team had anticipated trouble from disgruntled humans and drow, although the new cuffs used the kind of lightsilk that didn't burn the skin.

Ellis blinked when she saw the woman next to Mirelle. "Val?"

"Ellis." Val gave a sharp nod.

"What are you doing here?" Ellis asked. There was a pair of shadow magic goggles on Val's forehead. Ellis wasn't thrilled about that. There were certain technologies she didn't want humans to see yet. Val must have had a cloaker on, or she wouldn't have gotten past the security cordons.

"Look, kid, I've been planning for this day for years. I wasn't going to miss it. Although I, uh, hadn't planned on taking an active role."

Sebastian reached Ellis and stared at his former first mate. "Val," he growled.

"I think the words you're all looking for are 'Thank you,'" Val grumbled.

"Thank you," Ellis repeated quickly.

"What do we do with her?" one of the soldiers holding Val's arms asked.

"Let me go, kid," Val said. "Unless it's illegal to stop an assassination attempt."

"No, but sneaking past a military perimeter is. Arrest her for trespassing and take her to jail," Charlie ordered.

"You're going to let them do this?" Val asked Sebastian. "All of this is happening because of me!"

"This is a result that we miraculously pulled out of the chaos you caused," Sebastian corrected. "A lot of people died."

"It was for the greater good," Val insisted. The soldiers stripped her of the goggles and cloaker.

"Can I have those?" Ellis asked. Reluctantly, the soldiers handed her the devices. Raising one hand, she sent a wave of shadow magic toward the gear and dissolved it.

"Hey!" the soldier in command exclaimed, looking hungrily at the empty space between Ellis' hands. He'd sensed that he had found something valuable.

"It might have been booby-trapped," Ellis lied. "Safer this way."

"What do we do with the drow lady?" he asked.

"Put her in one of the cells in the military staging area," Charlie suggested. "She's as good a test case for our new system of legal cooperation as any."

"Look at that, Val. You *are* making an active contribution," Ellis offered.

"Do *not* hurt her," Charlie added, staring down the soldier. "How we handle practical problems in these early days is just as important as what we do in there." He pointed at the building where they would hold the signing. "Do you understand?"

"Yes, sir," the man acknowledged, nodding gravely.

"You want us to hold off?" another soldier asked. "Run another sweep?"

"No." Ellis didn't expect more trouble. "Let's do this."

McMasters appeared at her side. "Oh, no, you don't. I am *not* letting you bleed on my peace treaty. We used very nice paper." When McMasters threaded a needle, Ellis bridled. "It's not bad enough for stitches, and you're not a medic."

"This is for your *suit*, Ellis," he corrected. When he was done, you could barely see the repair. Finally, they all headed inside.

Ellis was built for scaling buildings, helping old ladies, and menacing ne'er-do-wells with sharp objects. She was not built for smiling pleasantly with her hands folded in her lap, listening to speeches about cooperation and shared futures. The ache of the arrow wound in her arm kept her alert, however. *I'll have to tell Mirelle she was helpful.*

Finally, it was time for the signing. When it was her turn, Ellis rose, dipped the metal nib of a drow pen in a pot of mushroom ink, and scrawled her name below her father's. As she formed the letters on the page, a deep, profound pride rose within her. She thought she heard shadowy laughter deep beneath her feet.

The last person to sign was General Jarwell. When he was done, he tucked the pen into his breast pocket, then straightened and addressed the solemn crowd. "Let's cap off this momentous day with a party."

It was the best night of Ellis' life. While waiters circled

with appetizers and champagne, a group of drow musicians gave a short performance. Drow music was very quiet, not meant for dancing. Ellis was astonished to learn that the Marines had not only a terrific military band but a very good deejay. Much to Landon's dismay, many handsome young officers invited Trissa to dance.

Later, waiters circlulated with silver trays bearing mini shrimp cocktails and tunnel bar squares. Rami had been invited to attend the ball as a guest but had insisted on catering the event. He claimed that food was very important for bringing people together, and in the end, he was right. The American diplomatic mission appeared to take it as a solemn duty to sample every variety of mushroom wine the drow delegation had brought. Repeatedly.

Even Percy seemed to be having a good time. Anyone favored by Rose's brilliant smile would have a good time, Ellis thought. Then she saw him standing next to General Jarwell. They were talking in low voices.

"What do you think they're talking about?" Ellis asked Charlie. He finished chewing a cube of marinated cave goat and dropped the toothpick on his plate.

"Percy's probably asking about Jarwell's ferret." Ellis didn't understand and had to wheedle Charlie into telling her the story. A slow song began, and Ellis wrapped her arms around her lover.

"Speaking of pets, I'm moving home after this. If I inflict Mr. Muffins on another pet sitter, the Hague is going to come after me for crimes against humanity."

"Oh." Ellis' mood dampened. She had enjoyed living with Charlie in the cabins. "I'll miss you bringing me coffee." She tried to force a smile onto her face.

"I thought you could come with me," Charlie added. "You singlehandedly took down a shadow monster. I imagine you can handle one small, mildly homicidal orange cat."

"First, Mr. Muffins is not that small," Ellis corrected. "Second, I haven't done anything singlehandedly. I had a lot of help."

"You have to take *some* credit," Charlie insisted.

"Mmm. Some, yes." Ellis grinned.

"Well, what do you say? About moving in?" Charlie asked.

"It would be a long commute," Ellis mused. They were maintaining the camp as a base for diplomatic relations.

"Shorter on a motorcycle," Charlie countered. "You could supervise the construction of the new embassy."

The government had offered to rebuild the Outpost, but Ellis had turned them down. There were too many bad memories there. Instead, the drow were building an embassy in the tunnels beneath downtown Los Angeles.

"What about your fears about me being a drow? Aging differently? That kind of thing?"

"We don't have to figure everything out at once," Charlie replied. "This whole project is about humans and drow living together in harmony, right? We can set a shining example."

"Is that what is this about? Diplomacy?" Ellis poked him in the ribs.

Charlie winced. "Well, also, I love you."

Ellis tightened her arms around him. "I love you, too. Let's do it."

On the other side of the room, a spoon tapped a glass,

and the room filled with the noise. The band quieted, and everyone turned to Ilva, who had raised her glass.

"Leading my people in this peace process has been a great honor," Ilva began. Her eyes were glassy, and she swayed cheerfully.

"Is she tipsy?" Charlie whispered. Ellis smiled. Ilva did seem more effusive than usual.

"I would not be here without the work of someone very important," Ilva continued. She grasped Connor's hand, and Ellis smiled. She was glad to hear her father honored. Ilva continued, "We all owe a great debt to someone who put her life on the line time after time for peace. Who I am pleased to call a daughter. Join me in a toast to Ellis Burton!"

Ellis opened her mouth but found that she was unable to speak. A tear had formed in her eye, and she knuckled it out. She had waited a long time for a mother, and shockingly, she appeared to have stumbled into one. She sniffled as Charlie raised his glass, grinning.

"To Ellis Burton!" the crowd chorused.

There were more toasts after that, increasingly drunken. It felt like a great culmination, but as Ellis drank and ate and danced with Charlie, she knew this wasn't the end.

In the morning, she would wake up, and the real work would begin.

Get sneak peeks, exclusive giveaways, behind the scenes content, and more. PLUS you'll be notified of special **one day only fan pricing** on new releases.

Sign up today to get free stories.

Visit: https://marthacarr.com/read-free-stories/

AUTHOR NOTES: MARTHA CARR
WRITTEN AUGUST 28, 2024

I've started a project answering questions for my son about my life. I realized after last year's fifth round of cancer, and then chemo this time that he was expecting me to die sooner rather than later. It's been a lot for him to deal with and there isn't much I can do to make it better, except tell him stories that I can leave behind – eventually. Hopefully, a long time from now. I'm going to let you guys listen in as well.

My author notes right now are going to be answers to questions and all of you can get to know me better, too. Maybe inspire, maybe give you a laugh along the way.

Today's question is: If you could go back, what would you do differently?

This is a dangerous question because I could easily fall down a rabbit hole of changing way too much. I would pay more attention to learning something in school and less attention to boys. I would make my curly hair way curlier instead of eternally trying to straighten it. I'd celebrate how gangly and tall and cute I was instead of hunching over and trying to be invisible. I definitely would not have started weird diets at the age of fourteen and instead celebrated the body I showed up with and eaten what I wanted. That was never a problem till I made it into one. I would have chosen a college based only on what I wanted to pursue in life and not on where friends were going or what family thought was appropriate. What does that even mean? I would have waited to date someone, marry someone, who really saw me and appreciated me and someone I felt the same way about too. I would have listened to my own inner voice far more and headed toward the things I wanted to do, instead of veering off to the sides way too often to do what others thought I should be doing.

Oh the 'shoulds' of life. One big dumpster fire.

There's probably more but you get the idea.

It's probably true that I'm also looking at this from all the wrong angles. Despite everything that was stacked against me back then, and there was a lot, I rose up time and time again, determined to get to a destination that was more of my choosing. And I did that over and over again. I became a writer despite the family's loud and continuous objections. I became a national columnist despite being told that was impossible. I became a successful author despite the predictions. I met someone who seems to see me in all my glory and gives me the chin nod, or smiles with the lines deepening around his eyes, or reaches for my hand all the time.

What if the right question is what would I do more of now that I know better? I mean, what I really try to remind myself of all the time is that in ten years I'll think this age was pretty young and held a lot of potential. What did I do with that opportunity? Can I appreciate who I am right now? Can I at least give myself a break? That's what we're really talking about here. Otherwise, everything at every moment in every year I've been alive is so serious and the path to a good life is narrow and fraught with peril.

I'm going with the idea that life is full of really good stuff on a very, very wide road that has a million different ways of getting anywhere and what I end up with, chances are, will not even be what I was so sure I needed, not exactly at least, and will be better than what I was even hoping I'd get. That has also been true for me.

Instead, I'm going to keep looking at how I am treating myself and others. I'm out here doing my best to keep judgment out of things. To make room for people to be different in all the splendid ways. To be curious about what I can do, or want to do, and about others. To be of service without being a doormat. To have fun and join in, particularly if it looks a little ridiculous and to remember that bougie is so much fun, and community is even better. Love you. Love, Mom. More adventures to follow.

AUTHOR NOTES: MICHAEL ANDERLE

WRITTEN AUGUST 28, 2024

First, thank you very much for not only reading the book, but looking at our author notes here in the back.

Ten Years of Literary Shenanigans: A Journey

A decade. That's how long I've been at this writing gig. Ten years since I first deluded myself into thinking I could string words together in a semi-coherent manner. And you know what?

Somehow, it worked. Don't ask me how.

Picture this: August 2014. There I was, a bright-eyed, bushy-tailed wannabe author, hammering out 35,000 words of what would eventually become 'Death Becomes Her' (The Kurtherian Gambit Series). And then, in a stroke of what I can only describe as sheer brilliance (or idiocy, take your pick), I promptly shoved it in a digital drawer. Because apparently, finishing things is overrated.

For the next year or so, I did what I thought I needed to

do - I read. A lot. Not just for fun, mind you. Oh no, I was on a mission. A mission to capture that elusive "Wow, I love this scene!" feeling.

By some miracle (or cosmic joke), I eventually cracked the code of writing and selling stories. And now, here I am, rambling at you in these author notes, collaborating with the infinitely patient Martha, all because I took the time to figure out what makes a story tick.

It's surreal, really. From stuffing a half-baked manuscript in a digital drawer to having actual readers - yes, you masochists - who willingly spend their time with our stories. It's... well, it's something that I probably don't deserve.

I'm grateful, truly. Even if my writing sometimes makes me want to bang my head against the keyboard (a feeling you may share), knowing that you're out there reading it makes it worthwhile.

So here's to ten years of literary misadventures, to digital drawers that mercifully don't stay closed, and to readers like you who, for reasons beyond my comprehension, make it all worthwhile. May the next decade be filled with even more shenanigans, both on and off the page.

God help us all.
Until the next book,

Ad Aeternitatem,
Michael Anderle

P.S. If you're a glutton for punishment and want more of... whatever this is, don't forget to subscribe to my newsletter.

It's like these author notes, but with more typos. Check it out here: https://michael.beehiiv.com/

P.P.S. Is it too late to consider a career in professional napping? Asking for a friend.

BOOKS BY MARTHA CARR

Other Series in the Oriceran Universe:

THE LEIRA CHRONICLES
CASE FILES OF AN URBAN WITCH
SOUL STONE MAGE
THE KACY CHRONICLES
MIDWEST MAGIC CHRONICLES
THE FAIRHAVEN CHRONICLES
I FEAR NO EVIL
THE DANIEL CODEX SERIES
SCHOOL OF NECESSARY MAGIC
SCHOOL OF NECESSARY MAGIC: RAINE CAMPBELL
ALISON BROWNSTONE
FEDERAL AGENTS OF MAGIC
SCIONS OF MAGIC
THE UNBELIEVABLE MR. BROWNSTONE
DWARF BOUNTY HUNTER
ACADEMY OF NECESSARY MAGIC
MAGIC CITY CHRONICLES
ROGUE AGENTS OF MAGIC

OTHER BOOKS BY JUDITH BERENS

OTHER BOOKS BY MARTHA CARR

JOIN THE ORICERAN UNIVERSE FAN GROUP ON FACEBOOK!

BOOKS BY MICHAEL ANDERLE

Sign up for the LMBPN email list to be notified of new releases and special deals!

https://lmbpn.com/email/

For a complete list of books by Michael Anderle, please visit:

www.lmbpn.com/ma-books/

CONNECT WITH THE AUTHORS

Martha Carr Social

Website: http://www.marthacarr.com

Facebook: https://www.facebook.com/groups/MarthaCarrFans/

Michael Anderle Social

Website: http://lmbpn.com

Email List: https://michael.beehiiv.com/

https://www.facebook.com/LMBPNPublishing

https://twitter.com/MichaelAnderle

https://www.instagram.com/lmbpn_publishing/

https://www.bookbub.com/authors/michael-anderle

www.ingramcontent.com/pod-product-compliance
Lightning Source LLC
LaVergne TN
LVHW041917070526
838199LV00051BA/2644